The Friday Friendship Club

by Anne Brooke

The Friday Friendship Club by Anne Brooke

Chapter One

January

Leonora

Friday night, and Leonora was running late, as usual. Her boss had decided there was something urgent Leonora had to do, just as she was about to leave. She'd given him The Look, but he hadn't paid a blind bit of attention. So she'd been forced to fulfil the pointless task before grabbing her handbag and rushing out of the office.

She'd heard his shouted *thank you* just before the door clicked shut behind her, but she hadn't bothered to go back inside to acknowledge him. It would only have wasted time.

A quick text to her two partners in crime, Selena and Dorothea (Dotty or Dots for short), a grab at the only seat left on the tube (she failed), a hard stare at the gum-chewing goth who'd got there before her, and Leonora was on her way.

She'd known Selena and Dorothea since college, about *cough-cough* years ago now. They'd met at the hugely boring Hi-Tech Secretarial course, had bonded over bad coffee and the horrors of shorthand, and had never looked back. Now, they all worked in the big city and on the last Friday night of every month they met at their favourite bar in Covent Garden to catch up. They might have only been able to spare a couple of hours or so these days, particularly with the commute for herself and Dotts, but it was always time well spent.

Tonight, the tube journey to Charing Cross seemed stupidly long. This wasn't made any more bearable by the fact that nobody in Leonora's carriage seemed to have remembered to wash this morning. She often thought that the mark of a civilisation was how well or poorly it treated its travelling citizens. In this regard, the UK looked set to fail pretty damn spectacularly very soon.

So, by the time Embankment station finally turned up, Leonora was desperate to get off the train. She only made it by a matter of seconds before the doors closed again. The angry glare she gave the man who'd not moved for her until the last minute went unnoticed as he was too busy staring at his phone. Typical.

No time to complain, as Leonora needed to get a move on or the girls would start without her. She ran up the little road to Charing Cross, clutching her handbag to her chest, and then turned right onto the Strand.

From there she hotfooted it past the crowds of people chatting, the groups of beggars, the shops and the theatre, and made it to the pub in record time. Thank goodness she never wore high heels to the office. She could never walk in the bloody things, let alone run. And, working in London as Leonora did, she liked to be able to have the option of running if circumstances dictated it. Mind you, every so often it would be good to have access to a good solid pair of stilettos for the sole purpose of beating people she didn't like over the head until they saw sense. Her boss for one.

Covent Garden was its usual mix of milling groups, confused tourists and street performers, including a juggler dressed entirely in yellow and two women turning cartwheels to general applause. Leonora ignored them all, turned down one of the old market streets and found her way to the set of stairs she was heading for. She could already hear the hubbub of conversation coming from the floor below. The Crusting Pipe wine bar had been their meeting venue for years.

She clattered down the stairs, scanning the tables outside the main bar area to see if she could spot her two favourite girlfriends. They were bound to be here as they preferred the outside area, and the pub had helpfully set up several enormous heaters to ensure nobody died of hypothermia. It was working as the tables were crammed with people – she'd never known the Pipe be empty – but Leonora was only halfway down when a hand shot up from a table at the edge and began waving frantically to attract her attention.

"Leonora! We're *over here!*" Selena's voice cut through the noise like a whistle at a football match and Leonora raised her hand in an answering wave and grinned in her direction. That girl would have been a brilliant sergeant major in another life – Selena had a voice that could strip paint without even being in the same room. Always a great skill for a woman.

The moment Leonora arrived, Selena leapt up and wrapped her in a huge hug which all but took her breath away.

"So good to see you!" Selena said. "And happy birthday in advance for tomorrow. Here's your gift. It's from us both."

With that, her friend let her go, pulled out a chair for Leonora and produced an enormous bag which she plonked in the middle of the table. Dorothea poured Leonora a much-needed glass of white and pushed it in her direction.

"Good to see you," Dotts said with a warm smile. "I'm afraid I couldn't stop Selena buying this for you, so I had no option but to go halves on it. However, I've got the receipt if you need it."

Leonora couldn't help but laugh. Sometimes she thought her two closest friends would make a great comedy duo: Selena with her over-the-top enthusiasm and built-in zest for life, set against the quieter and more thoughtful Dotty. She herself was somewhere in the middle though she could go completely over-the-top every now and then. Thank goodness for Dotty for bringing them down to earth when they most needed it. It was funny how their friendship had lasted through the years, and meeting up with them always made her feel better. Selena gave her a sense of hope and Dotty gave her a sense of perspective – both vital attributes in the modern world.

Leonora took a swig from her glass before she tackled the package. Her wine tasted bright and oaky and made her think of summer holidays on warm, wide beaches. Just what she could do with right now. Then she opened the parcel and peered inside. She started to laugh. "What the hell!"

Slowly, Leonora began pulling out the items. It was easy to tell this was Selena's idea alone as no way on earth would Dotty have ever considered this.

First out of the bag came a bright red camisole with a front made entirely of lace. Once on, it would leave nothing to the imagination. Then Leonora found a matching pair of knickers that looked as if they'd disappear up the crack the moment she breathed, never to be seen again. Underneath these was a very sparkly set of handcuffs and a small box carefully wrapped in tissue. As she took each item out of the bag and laid it on the table, Selena's laughter grew ever louder, at about the same rate as Dotty's groans.

"Do you have to take them out of the bag?" Dotty whispered, as she glanced round the courtyard. "People might see."

Leonora gave her girlfriends a look. "Isn't that the point? You know half the fun for you is me opening my presents. I wouldn't want to deprive you."

Dotty gave a wry smile. "Don't you mean half the fun for Selena? For heaven's sake, don't count me in!"

"But of course. Though didn't you just admit you paid for half of it?"

"Hmm," she replied. "A good point well made. I think Selena must have worn down my defences."

"Hey!" the subject of their conversation replied. "You were more than happy to pay your share. And anyway, what's not to like about all this? It's ideal for a woman in her prime. These are our sexual years, don't you know."

This didn't sound like anything Selena might have found in a genuine scientific study. "Have you been reading *Red* magazine again?"

"Might have been," Leonora's craziest friend admitted with a pout. "They know what they're talking about. You should definitely be listening to them."

For a moment or two, there seemed to be something serious in Selena's reply, but when Leonora gave her a questioning glance, she smiled innocently back. Dotty in the meantime rolled her eyes and took a sip of her wine.

Leonora opened the final box and blinked. "Are these what I think they are?"

"Yes!" Selena replied, punching the air with her fist. "Anal beads and nipple clamps. Just what every prime-time woman needs to reinvent her sex life."

Once again, Leonora had to laugh. Mainly because Selena's voice levels didn't have a whisper button and her statement had reached at least three sets of tables next to them. At this rate, Leonora wasn't sure they'd be allowed back into their favourite pub again. Mind you, she always had the impression they pretty much welcomed everything here in Covent Garden so if she decided to use the nipple clamps right now and dance naked round the courtyard in all her glory, they might not have batted an eyelid. Or anything else.

The issue she was desperately trying to ignore was this: she wasn't sure anal beads and nipple clamps would ever see any action this side of the next millennium. Bedroom relations with her husband were thin on the ground these days. And they'd used to be so good together in that way too. Leonora loved everything about Bob and always had done, from the very beginning. She'd always felt they were a team: she and her husband against the whole world, if need be. They supported each other.

And they still did. But, lately, Bob was just so busy at work helping to set up accounts for a new company and was working such ridiculous hours that he had no energy for anything other than eating, watching TV and sleeping. In fact, Leonora couldn't remember the last time she'd had any action in the bedroom. Maybe she should at the very least get that camisole on and give Bob something he would keep awake for. That sounded like a plan.

"Thank you both for these very imaginative gifts," she said. "I promise you I won't be letting you know on any level how I get on with them."

"Thank goodness for that," said Dotty, raising her glass in Leonora's direction.

"Spoilsport!" protested Selena, but she quietened down when Leonora leant forward to refill her wine. "How is Bob, by the way?"

Leonora sighed and repeated what she'd just been thinking. "Working all the hours to help get this new company set up. It's not fair but he's the one with all the accounts experience. And of course he's done set-ups before."

This was true. Bob had been working for the same accountancy firm for fifteen years and had helped three or four new companies get their accounts systems and international tax details right. He'd explained the whole process to Leonora about a thousand times, but she didn't have a brain for numbers so it had never made any sense to her. She usually had some idea what these new companies did though – she remembered one had been a perfume maker, another an artist who gave art lessons in old people's homes and still another had been setting up a charity for helping young mothers. She couldn't remember what the current new set-up did, though Bob must have told her at some point. He always did. Turning fifty-five tomorrow meant Leonora's memory was shot to pieces. Much like her hormones.

She wondered what her husband would be giving her for her birthday. She'd dropped enough hints over the last few weeks. She wondered if it would be the pearl-and-diamond earrings she'd seen in their local jewellery shop. They were tiny but very beautiful. But, failing that, she would be happy with either the Yves St Laurent Black Opium perfume she loved to wear or a £50 voucher for their local beauty salon. A woman could dream anyway – hell, if Leonora was being honest, she'd be satisfied with a card and a bottle of champagne, just as long as he remembered. She wasn't a high-maintenance wife.

As she continued to work her way through the bottle of white with Selena and Dotty, Leonora caught up with what was going on in the very different worlds of her two best friends.

Selena owned an independent costume workshop in west London. She made a lot of money creating costumes for theatres across the country, and also had a hugely popular following on YouTube. She'd always been the artistic one of the three of them and Leonora had no idea why she'd bothered with a secretarial qualification in the first place. She was sure Selena had never used it though she was more than glad her friend had gone on the course to get those typing skills, as Leonora would never have met her otherwise. She gazed fondly at Selena now as she gave them the low-down of her month and how she thought she might have a new client from America. Her bright red hair (dyed) shone out like a beacon on this damp January night and her hands danced patterns in the air as she spoke. Leonora had never known anyone with as much energy and simple love of life as Selena. Whenever things were bad, she always managed to cheer everyone up.

"So," Selena was saying, "I had an email from this American theatre company director a few weeks ago and assumed it was spam. I mean what would America want with me? They've got Hollywood and more costume suppliers than you could poke a needle at. So I ignored it. Then last week I had a phone call at what must have been the middle of the night for them – though the time differences are a mystery to me. Apparently, he saw my YouTube channel and wants to get in touch about the costumes for a play his company are doing in the spring. In London. He's going to send me the details. It's all a bit last minute but I'm going to put together a portfolio of pictures which might fit the brief. It's very difficult to tell. Theatre directors are always mad."

She paused to take a gulp of wine, and Leonora and Dotty smiled at each other. Selena calling someone else mad had a distinct whiff of *pot*, *kettle* and *grimy*, but they were far too sensible to suggest it out loud.

"What's the play they're doing?" Dotty asked, still trying to suppress her smile.

"Oh, *The Importance of Being Earnest*," Selena replied, waving her wine glass around as if she might be about to conduct an orchestra with it. "Which is totally surreal as it's the archetypal English play. Not sure what an American will make of it. I suppose if I get the project, I'll find out soon enough. But, anyway, enough about me. How have things been going for you, Dotts? Only as much as you're allowed to tell us though!"

Dotty pursed her lips and gave a slight shake of her head. She never liked them teasing her about her civil service job. Whenever they asked her about it, her replies would be kept to general details about office meetings and the busyness of work. She'd never said exactly what she did, except it was administration and 'not very important'.

Selena had often wondered out loud if Dotty might be a spy, but Leonora had laughed that off as being over-dramatic. She herself knew from experience that administration was exactly how it sounded. Still, it was funny how Dotty never really said anything about it. Selena and Leonora moaned about work all the time. Dotty was different. She was a very private person and had been ever since they'd known her.

Leonora smiled at her, admiring her neat chestnut-brown hair and her smart grey suit. She'd never known Dotty be anything less than well turned-out. She sometimes wondered if her friend woke up looking as if she was totally prepared for the morning. Unlike herself, who woke up looking as if she'd been involved in a night-long battle (usually with the duvet) and hadn't ended up on the winning side. Dotty was also Bob's sister, and therefore Leonora's sister-in-law, but was utterly different from him in every way.

"Things are fine," said Dotty. "It's been much the same month as it usually is. We're thinking of taking on some work experience students over the summer so that's new. The big boss is keen on showing how interesting a career in the civil service can be. Which means he's given it to me to sort out."

"Wow!" Selena chipped in. "New spies, then?"

Dotty groaned. "No. You mean new unpaid labour and a chance for everyone to offload their filing, don't you?"

"Yes," Leonora said, giving Selena a firm stare. "That's exactly what she means. It's the wine talking, Dotty."

"It so isn't," Selena protested. "I've not had nearly enough yet. I could order another bottle or …"

"Or …?" Leonora prompted her when it looked as if Selena wasn't going to finish her suggestion any time soon.

Her friend turned to her with a look of determined delight. "Or we could have an unexpectedly early night just this once and promise faithfully to have a longer session next month."

Leonora laughed. "Why? Why would we want to do that?"

"Because," Selena explained, "if you go home early, you can make the best use of your birthday gifts to start your weekend off as you mean to go on."

Dorothea put her hands over her ears. "You're talking about my brother here," she pleaded.

But, by now, Selena was unstoppable. "Yes! It's a brilliant idea. You can dash home, try on that camisole set, add on the nipple clamps and do whatever you'd like to do with the beads. You can make it a birthday to really remember! Bob won't know what's hit him. Oh, and let us know afterwards how you got on. You can thank me later!"

Leonora, still laughing at Selena's sheer enthusiasm, was about to refuse and continue with the evening they'd planned. But then, to her own surprise, she thought: why not? She was going to be fifty-five tomorrow. Perhaps it was time to try something new and, at the same time, get her marriage back on track. There was no need to wait for Bob to finish his project. She could take the marital power into her own hands and show him exactly how much she loved him. Being subtle and supportive hadn't helped her love life lately, so it was time to be a little bit wilder.

So, Leonora stood up.

"I think you're right," she said. "I'm going to do exactly that. I know you might not have been expecting me to take that suggestion seriously, but actually I'm going to do it."

Dotts looked up at her in horror. Even Selena raised her eyebrows, and then nodded.

"Good for you," she said. "Not what I was expecting but you go, girl! I hope everything goes wonderfully for you both. You'll definitely have a birthday you'll never forget!"

"I hope so too," Leonora replied, unable to keep the smile from her lips. "We'll catch up properly next time, I promise. And I'll text you and let you know when I'm home. You two stay and finish that bottle."

Leonora gave them both a heartfelt hug, gathered up her belongings, not forgetting the bag of presents she hoped to make use of later tonight, and trotted out of the courtyard and up the stairs. At the top, she turned back and waved at her friends just as Selena gave her a huge wolf-whistle. She was the only woman Leonora had ever known who could do that.

Meanwhile, Leonora's mind was buzzing with her unexpected change of plans for the night. Whatever happened, she would be sailing into her fifty-fifth birthday with style. Bob wouldn't be able to believe his luck.

All these thoughts and more filled her head as she made her way back through the bright lights of London to Waterloo Station. By dint of running up the station escalators (verdict: bloody exhausting but Leonora was sure it would be worth it) and hot-footing it across the main concourse, she managed to get onto a train that would get her home by 9pm. She'd thought about grabbing a burger on her way through the station but there hadn't been time and she could always have something to eat at home. Once they'd done the naughty stuff she was planning.

Leonora half-wondered about texting Bob to see if he could pick her up early, but that would spoil everything. No, she'd get a taxi and give her husband the surprise of his life. She would put on her best sultry expression (Leonora wasn't sure what one of those actually was but she was determined to make a good go of it), wave the camisole set in his direction, add some sexy music to the mix and then … well, then she'd give Bob her full attention in every way and see what came up. As it were. She'd have to remember to nip to the bathroom first and use her secret Vaseline supply – at her age, Leonora needed a bit of forward planning in the downstairs department. She might even crack open some champagne afterwards to get her special weekend off to a flying start.

Forty minutes or so later, she arrived at her local station. It was only a fifteen-minute walk to get home, but Leonora had already decided to get a taxi. It wasn't prime taxi time so she had the opportunity to text Selena and Dotty that she was nearly home now. Selena's response came in immediately.

Have fun, glamour girl! Selena messaged, and Leonora sent a thumbs-up reply. Two minutes later, a taxi turned up and she grabbed it. Though the taxi didn't have a lot of choice as she was the only one in the queue. Nobody else had come home this early on a Friday night.

"Where to, madam?" said the driver as Leonora settled herself and her bags into the back of his cab. When she told him, he nodded and set off.

A few minutes later and they were turning into the road she and Bob lived in. They'd moved here ten years ago from the main town about five miles away as they'd been after a bigger garden and more space. Not that they needed the space as they didn't have any children, by choice. But when Bob got an unexpected but well-deserved promotion, he decided he wanted a study to enable him to do more work at home, so they'd eventually found this house after several months of searching and one or two near-misses.

At the time, the near-misses had been heartbreaking, but now Leonora was glad they'd ended up here. The road was a no-through one, so there wasn't a great deal of traffic, which she loved. It meant she could sit in the garden during summer and be totally at peace. In their old house, that hadn't been possible and she hadn't realised how much peace and quiet mattered until they moved. Or maybe that was her age – it was hard to tell. Still, fifty-five in a few hours' time was nothing, was it? Fifty-five was the new thirty-five and, starting right now, she was going to make the most of it.

Leonora gave the taxi driver a generous tip and he waved at her as he turned round and headed back the way into town. As she tottered down the path with her precious bags, she saw the bedroom light was on. Opening the front door, the hall was in darkness. At the same time, Leonora became aware of strange sounds coming from upstairs. Groans and muffled laughter. Bob must be watching porn on the laptop. Stifling her own laughter and growing excitement, Leonora decided she didn't want to cramp his style, but she most definitely wanted to join in. That would make his day. At the very least it would give him the kind of big finish he hadn't expected.

Leaving her bags on the hall floor and softly clicking the front door shut, Leonora grabbed Selena's present and tip-toed to the downstairs loo. She whipped off her work suit and replaced it with the camisole set. Then checking her appearance in the mirror, she went out into the hallway again, located the shoe cupboard (yes, they really did have one!), fumbled about in the dark for her one pair of killer high heels and put them on.

Then she crept up the stairs, as the sounds of Bob's porn channel became ever louder (whoever this particular starlet was, she knew what she wanted), and arrived at the bedroom door. Bob was going to get such a surprise. Then Leonora smoothed down her hair and pushed open the door, at the same time saying in as sex-kitten a voice as she could manage, "Darling! I'm home, and ready for action!"

What she saw when she entered the bedroom was for one astonishingly long moment a complete mystery to her. In fact, Leonora remembered thinking how odd it was that the woman from the porn video Bob was watching had somehow made it into their bedroom, and onto their bed. And then she remembered telling herself how utterly stupid she was being.

The woman on the bed was on top of her husband and was bouncing up and down with all the enthusiasm of a puppy being given its first treat. She had long blonde hair tied up into a ponytail and a tattoo of a flower on her right bum-cheek. She couldn't have been more than mid thirties.

That was all Leonora could take in before she started screaming. She raced towards the bed and grabbed the woman by that bloody ponytail. At the same time, Bob was trying to get out from underneath. He didn't need to try too hard as Leonora had already pulled the woman backwards and shoved her onto the floor.

"Take your hands off me, you crazy bitch!" the woman yelled at Leonora, her accent more estuary than downtown Surrey.

"Get away from my husband!" Leonora yelled back.

"What the hell are you doing home?" Bob yelled, proving beyond doubt that he hadn't yet grasped the whole horror of this incident.

"What the hell are you doing with *her*?" Leonora screamed in reply.

"It's just a one-off!" her husband shouted, finally getting with the programme. "I'm sorry!"

As Leonora turned to respond to Bob, the woman pushed herself off the floor and faced them both down, not seeming to care that she was completely naked. She was beautiful. At once Leonora felt how flabby her own thighs and how small her own breasts were in comparison.

"A one-off?" the woman yelled. "That's a lie! I've been shagging your husband for six months and you still haven't worked it out. Anyway, he doesn't want to have sex with you so why not leave the field clear for me? And seeing how stupid you look right now in that get-up, who can blame him? Talk about mutton dressed as lamb!"

"You bitch!" Leonora yelled and went for the woman's hair once more.

The woman fought back, kicking and spitting at Leonora. Bob started yelling and tried to pull them apart, but Leonora wasn't having any of it. She'd had enough.

"Get out!" she yelled. "Get out, the both of you!"

With that, Leonora stopped pulling the naked woman's hair and started instead to push her out of the room. At the same time, she grabbed Bob and began pulling him in the direction of the door.

"Stop it, Leonora!" Bob said, quietly, but somehow his words reached her. "We're going, we're going. *I'm sorry.*"

Leonora stopped and took a few steps back. For a moment it didn't matter that he and the other woman were both naked and it didn't matter how stupid she herself must have looked. It was for that moment just Leonora and him, and this terrible thing happening in their marriage.

"Get out," Leonora said again, just as quietly as her husband had spoken, but with the most intent she'd ever had in her whole life. "*Sorry* doesn't cut it. Just go."

Another long moment and then he nodded. Suddenly Leonora was the most tired she'd ever been. Bob turned and began scooping up clothes from the foot of the bed.

"Give us a minute and we'll be gone," he said.

"Make sure you are."

With that, Leonora left the bedroom. The moment she was on the landing, a fierce but whispered conversation between Bob and the woman began. Leonora ignored it and marched downstairs, seething with fury. Everything seemed jagged, on edge, as if she'd dived into a pool expecting warmth and encountered only ice. In the hallway, she grabbed her coat and shoved it over her stupid camisole before shaking off the high heels and kicking them into the corner. She couldn't stop trembling. She walked into the living room and then into the kitchen and back to the living room again. Her eyes were hot with tears and she wiped one hand angrily across them, trying not to think.

The sound of a slamming door from upstairs and then she heard footsteps. Leonora walked back out into the hallway and watched as Bob and the other woman came down the stairs. They were wearing clothes, thank God.

Bob saw her and started to say something, but Leonora shook her head.

"I don't have anything to say to you," she said. "Just get out, please."

"Okay," Bob replied. "Okay. We'll talk later, Leonora. And once again I'm sorry."

But she didn't want to hear that. She didn't want to hear any of it.

"Oh just fuck off!" she yelled.

"That's exactly what we plan to do," said the woman, pushing one hand through her hair. *"Loser."*

And then, before Leonora could respond, she and Bob were gone, the front door slamming shut behind them.

For several moments, Leonora stood in the hallway, staring at the door and feeling the wild pounding of her heart.

Then she turned as if in a trance. She walked carefully into the living room again, sat down on the sofa, put her head in her hands and began to sob as if she would never be able to stop.

Chapter Two

January

Selena

Everyone thought Selena was at best a little eccentric and at worst totally insane. She'd grown used to this early on in life and had mainly dreamt her way through school, doing the bare minimum possible in her lessons. Except art, which had gripped her and taken over her whole soul almost before she even understood what colours could be.

Because colours were all-embracing. They swooped in and made you think differently about everything. They were the ground beneath Selena's feet and the air she lived in. They were the beginning and end of her life. She could find them anywhere: in pencils and in crayons; in buildings and in trees; in people and in animals. And she could feel the emotions and heart behind every colour she came across.

Blue was a shy colour, though the darker it was, the more its confidence grew. When she used blue in her designs, Selena gave voice to the subtle side of her nature – which did exist, no matter what people said. Orange, on the other hand, was the colour of hope. Nobody could be near anything orange and not feel a little lift of excitement as to what the future might bring.

Yellow could be mean, but that didn't matter as its very meanness brought out the power of any colour she matched it with. It could be moody too, and change its mind, even about its very nature. Sometimes even the meanest colour could be kind, like people.

Red was the colour of love, and you had to be very careful when it came to love. Red couldn't be trusted, though it might well give you the best experience you could ever have. Selena treated red with great respect and didn't even like to turn her back on it. Sometimes red could rend you into pieces, heart and bone, and you had to treat it like fire.

Selena had grown up knowing all this about the world, without needing to put it into words. It was perhaps because of this that she'd never found her tribe at school. It was only when she'd gone to college (on a whim as she hadn't been bothered either way) and met Leonora and Dotty that something inside her had clicked. She had been attracted to their colours. Leonora was blue with flashes of orange – shyness with an enchanting undercurrent of hope. On the other hand, Dotty was somewhere between silver and brown, with the softest of pinks floating its way through when you least expected it – formality with a deep vein of kindness. This hope and kindness had first called to Selena in college, and its grip had never weakened.

However, sometimes she wondered if the three of them had stayed friends all these years partly because they were each happily child-free. The world was full of families, but there were some – such as herself – who stood apart from that particular calling. The same was true of her two special friends. In any case, whatever the many different reasons behind their friendship, being with Leonora and Dotty made Selena feel at home in her skin.

All these thoughts and memories were filling Selena's head when she woke up on the morning of Leonora's birthday. She hoped Leonora had had a marvellous time with Bob last night and was glad her friend had been inspired by the gift they'd given her. Recently she'd sensed all might not be well in Leonora's marriage, so Selena congratulated herself that perhaps her present had made things easier in that respect. She would make sure to find out all about it later. Or as much as Leonora would tell her anyway.

In the bathroom, Selena took a moment – as she always did – to admire the décor. Her bathroom was a vision in green and yellow, with the fittings in a paler yellow she'd had to search high and low for. These were the colours of nature and sunshine, and gave an inspirational start to her day. She'd put up the tiles herself, creating a random pattern of green and yellow splashes across the walls. It had taken her ages, but it had been so worth it.

She was humming as she stripped off her pyjamas and headed straight to the shower. She started off with an invigorating blast of icy cold water which made her shriek but it didn't matter as there was nobody to hear. Then she turned the temperature up as far as possible for as many seconds as she could bear it before bringing it back down to a heat she could actually wash in.

Back in the bedroom, Selena opened her enormous wardrobe which was arranged entirely by colour. After a moment of contemplation, she picked a bright lemon-yellow jersey top which was jostling for attention, and matched it with an orange-and-green striped skirt and a pale grey and fairly thick scarf that would help the bright colours to sing. Selena knew perfectly well how her friends expected her to be clashing in the colours she wore, but in fact she never chose colours that truly clashed. The arguments between them would be overwhelming and she wouldn't be able to think. No, she chose colours that were always magnificent together and showed other people how truly wonderful the world could be.

Outerwear selected, Selena turned her attention to her underwear. Not wanting the skirt or the top to feel they had competition, she picked a light grey matching bra and knicker set – in silk, of course – and got dressed. A pair of large glittering costume jewellery earrings and a couple of silver bangles completed the ensemble, and Selena pronounced herself satisfied with the look.

She smiled at her wardrobe before closing it as she didn't want any of the other outfits to feel left out. That would never do. If the colours ever started fighting – *really* fighting – then who knew what would happen?

Grimacing at the very thought, Selena grabbed her phone and her bag and went downstairs. She desperately needed a coffee. She switched on the coffee maker and took a couple of defrosted croissants out of the fridge where she'd had the foresight to put them yesterday morning. She'd been in no state to remember anything domestic last night.

After the first few gulps of coffee had warmed her through, she took her phone (so gorgeous in its sexy pink cover!) and deactivated the silent button. She didn't like to start her days with a beeping phone and left this task until after breakfast was done.

The moment Selena turned her silent switch off and gave her mobile some attention, she saw she had three or four new phone calls, all of them from Leonora, and no less than two messages.

Selena listened to the first message and then, with a growing sense of alarm, to the other message as well. Both of these were from Leonora and had come through in the very early hours of this morning. Neither of them made any sense, mainly because her friend was crying so much. She had no idea what Leonora was saying.

She rang her friend at once and her call was picked up after two rings.

"Leonora?" Selena said, her heart pounding. "It's me, Selena. Is that you? Are you all right? What's going on?"

"It's Bob," Leonora replied, her voice so low that it took a moment for Selena to work out what she was saying. "He was with someone. He's left. With her. I pushed them both out. He was in our bed, Selena. *In our bed.*"

Selena couldn't take it in. She shook her head to try to clear her thoughts. "I'm coming, Leonora. I'm coming to see you. *Now*. I'll grab some things and I'll be on my way. I'll be with you as soon as I can. Don't go anywhere until I arrive. I'll text you when I'm on the train. I'll come and we'll talk. We all love you, Leonora. I'll be with you soon."

The only reply from Leonora was more sobbing, a sound which tore at Selena's heart and at the same time made her absolutely furious with bloody Bob. If that bloody man was here right now, she'd punch him into the middle of next month, let alone next week. What an arse!

Selena turned off the coffee maker, grabbed her bag and a coat for the journey, then hesitated, galloped back to the kitchen and stuffed her handbag full of chocolate. Leonora was bound to need chocolate. And wine too, but it was too early for wine, even for them. Selena could go out and get some later once she was at her friend's house.

Chocolate sorted, she hurried to the front door and flung it open. There she gasped as she came face to face with a tall brown-haired man wearing a dark blue shirt and cream chinos who somehow, in that first instant, was surrounded with all the colours of the rainbow and more. She blinked and the colours eased their intensity and drifted into the normal sights she expected to see at her front door: the neighbour's fence, her garden path, the trees on the other side of the road. The man remained, however, so he was definitely not a figment of her imagination.

"Hello," she said. "Who are you? And whoever you are, I don't have time for anything. I'm on an emergency mission to a friend and that's the most important thing of all."

Unexpectedly, her visitor gave her a wide grin which lit up his whole face and made his sparkly brown eyes even more sparkly. Must be a trick of the light, Selena thought, or the effect of too much wine last night.

"Good for you," the stranger said, the lilt of his American accent obvious. "Friends are all important so I won't keep you. I'm assuming you're Selena MacPherson, the theatre costume lady?"

Selena nodded as she stepped outside and closed the front door behind her. "Yes. That's me. What can I do for you? Whatever it is, it had better be quick!"

"No problem," the man replied and began to trot alongside her as she hurried in the direction of the station. "I'm Max Nicholson, the theatre producer you've been talking to online. About our play and your fabrics."

"Oh, of course you are!" Selena replied, as it suddenly became clear. "You're the only American I know. I wasn't expecting to see you until next week."

"Yes, I know, but I had a couple of meetings cancelled so I thought I'd check where your workshop is. Then, as I was here, I thought I'd call by to see if we could chat. You said you lived opposite your business in one of your emails so I'm glad I chose the right house."

One of the many joys of Selena's workshop was that it was just opposite her home so her morning commute was ridiculously short. When her business really started to take off about five years ago, she'd quickly outgrown the spare rooms in her house so had looked around for space for an office and workshop not too far away. It hadn't taken long for her to find that the two-bedroom flat opposite hers was up for rent and had the kind of large windows she'd always dreamed of having. She'd checked with the landlord that it was okay to run a business from there, got the go-ahead and signed the papers within a week. It had been a miracle and she could hardly believe her luck.

Now, Selena visited her precious workshop every day, even when she wasn't planning to do any work. It was where she felt happiest. There was something about the calmness of the light and the way it interacted with the fabrics and colours that made her feel both rested and inspired. A good combination of feelings for a designer. She was convinced that in her workshop she could hear the voices of the colours more clearly than anywhere else on the planet.

However, no matter how keen she might be on chatting things through with her surprise visitor, right now she had a train to catch and a friend to support.

"That's great," she said to Max as he continued to keep pace with her. "It's lovely to meet you and, honestly, I'd love nothing more than to spend time with you talking about designs, but are you still okay to have our meeting on Monday? 2.30pm, isn't it?"

"Yes, sure," he replied, not even out of breath though Selena herself was panting with the effort of half-running and talking at the same time. "Happy to do that. I'll be at your workshop then. Oh, and good luck with visiting your friend."

"Thank you!" Selena replied and gave Max a wave as she reached the tube station before disappearing down into its cavernous depths. Unexpectedly, she found she was smiling.

The train journey from London to downtown Surrey where Leonora lived was much as the train journey always was, though with fewer people due to it being a weekend. She texted her friend to say she was on the train but didn't get a reply. Instead, Selena took the time to have another quick look at the requirements for Max's theatre project on her phone and then wondered if she should text Dotty and let her know what was happening. Though, probably, Leonora would have already contacted Dotts and, in any case, it wasn't Selena's story to tell. No, she'd wait until she got to Leonora's and see how things were then. The problem of Bob being Dotty's brother gave rise to a whole other level of complications. Dotty might already know about what Bob was up to, if it wasn't just a really untimely one-night stand. *Might she have known and not told Leonora?*

No! Dotty wasn't like that – she'd be in as much of a state of shock as Selena was, she was sure of it.

Leonora was the only one of the three of them who was married, and Selena had always assumed her marriage was a good one. Well, up unto recently, when she'd wondered whether her friend and her husband might be going through a bad patch. Selena had thought this because Leonora hadn't been as expansive as usual about Bob's many – and mostly amusing – faults. In fact, for the last couple of times the three of them had met up, Leonora had waved away polite enquiries about how Bob was and had just said he was fine. That wasn't like her. Part of the sheer enjoyment of Leonora being married to Dotty's brother had been making fun of Bob, in a good way.

Here and now, Selena didn't feel like making fun of Bob in a good way at all. Rather, she wanted to cut his body into tiny pieces using her second-best fabric scissors (not her best ones, oh no!) and stuff him down the nearest sewage system. Entirely without the use of anaesthetic. How could he cheat on Leonora like this? And in their own home too. The very thought of it made Selena's gut twist with suppressed rage from which all the colours of black and scarlet swirled around in a wild whirlpool. She had to keep calm – she was going to see Leonora to support her, not to stir her up to fury – so Selena closed her eyes and tried to focus on calming colours, such as pink and cream and white. After a while she felt a smidgeon better, but the fury was still there at her heart and didn't seem like it was going to leave her any time soon.

Before she knew it, Selena had arrived at the station where Leonora lived. She leapt off the train and ran for a taxi. She was in luck and managed to bag the second cab in the line, having been beaten to the first one by a very determined elderly lady with a large umbrella and a hell of a lot of attitude.

In the taxi, Selena took out her mobile and texted her friend. Once again, there was no answer, but in all honesty Selena didn't expect one. Poor Leonora had far too much on her mind. What a nightmare. Bloody, *bloody* Bob. Why couldn't he keep it in his trousers, especially this weekend? *On his wife's birthday.* He was a total fool. In Selena's secret opinion, Leonora was way out of Bob's league and always had been. Bob had been lucky to land her.

At Leonora's house, Selena paid the fare with a generous tip and sprang out of the taxi. She hurried down the path and pressed the front-door bell. She could hear the sing-song echoes inside the house but there was no answering footstep in the hallway. Leonora had to know it was her.

She banged on the door, and shouted, all the colours of red and purple spitting a rising worry through her mind. "Leonora, it's me! I'm here. Are you okay?"

A few anxious heartbeats later and the front door opened. Leonora looked exhausted, with dark shadows under her eyes as if she'd not slept all night.

"Oh, Leonora," Selena whispered. "I'm so, so sorry."

And then she dropped her bag on the path, opened her arms wide and hugged Leonora with all the strength she possessed. It was going to be a long and difficult day.

Chapter Three

January

Dorothea

Dorothea couldn't, by any stretch of the imagination, be described as a lover of parties. She was more of a stay inside and read a good book kind of woman. This had meant she'd not made many friends at school or college, except for Leonora and Selena. She'd found herself swept up into being part of their friendship group because they'd sat next to each other at college, but she'd been so startled by Selena's sheer joie de vivre and moved by Leonora's belief that the lives ahead of them would be good ones that she'd been quite happy to be part of the trio. And she'd been both delighted and astonished at how their friendship had lasted over the years. It was a blessing she'd never expected to have.

At college, Dorothea had worked steadily and done well at her exams. The trouble was she'd not had a particular career aim in mind at any point in her life and, even now in her mid-fifties, she sometimes wondered what she might like to be when she grew up.

That said, she really loved her job and couldn't imagine life without it.

She was quietly proud that she worked for the Civil Service. Yes, the commute was a long one from where she lived in Sussex but it had never worried her. The train travel gave a structure to her days which Dorothea enjoyed. It allowed her time for reading and thinking. Every so often, someone on the train would hold an informal evening class and Dorothea would occasionally join in with these. As a result, she had a smattering of holiday Italian, a vague understanding of ancient Greek philosophy and the first half of a scarf she'd never got round to finishing as the woman who'd been showing them how to crochet it had found another job nearer her home. Dorothea was fully determined to finish the scarf one day. She was simply waiting for the right time to do it.

Thinking of that unfinished scarf made her remember last night's almost-celebration with Leonora, and the meal she and Selena had shared when Leonora had rushed home. Selena, she was sure, would be able to finish the scarf in minutes and in the right colours too. But that wasn't the point. She herself would complete the scarf one day. Just not yet.

To distract herself, Dorothea glanced at her bedside clock. 6.45am, it told her in bright yellow figures. So already she'd had a lie-in of one hour and forty-five minutes, which was rather satisfying. However, if she left it much longer, she'd probably have a headache or be below par all day – which would be a waste of a good weekend.

With that in mind, she flung her duvet to one side and reached for her dressing-gown. Then she padded downstairs to make herself a morning tea. She didn't have time during the week so this was a treat just for herself. When she was commuting, Dorothea bought a tea at the station before she got on her train, but her own tea was always the best.

Her house wasn't huge – certainly not as large as Leonora's and nowhere near as interesting as Selena's – but it was hers and she loved it. A cosy two-bedroomed cottage in the centre of the village with a large back garden and a driveway just big enough for her car, it suited her needs perfectly and she loved its quirkiness. She'd fallen in love with it the moment she'd spotted it over fifteen years ago and had been thrilled when her offer had been accepted by the elderly couple who were selling up to move closer to their daughter and her family up in Hertfordshire. She'd been surprised to get the call from the estate agent, especially as she'd known her offer wasn't the highest one but it had been all she could afford at the time. However, she'd been the only cash buyer – due to savings she had from an inheritance from her parents – and this had sealed the deal.

Downstairs, the moment she opened the kitchen door, her cat Oscar came to wind himself around her legs, purring wildly.

"Yes, yes, I know," she said, leaning down to stroke his soft white fur. "You're dying of hunger."

Dorothea switched on the kettle before taking the tin of cat food from the pantry. She'd never expected to turn into a cat person. But she hadn't been able to refuse when her ex-neighbour had emigrated to New Zealand and had been desperate for someone to care for their beloved pet. She'd had Oscar for over four years now and these days he was a little stiffer when he walked – but then again nobody was getting any younger. Certainly not herself.

An hour later, and Oscar was sitting on her lap, purring away and kneading her skirt as she flicked through the paper. She thought she might do a little mending of the garden fence and then wander down to the village to check out the mobile library. There were always one or two interesting books to draw the eye. Then this afternoon she might try writing a little poetry if she was in the mood – it was a hobby she liked to indulge in every so often. One day a long time from now someone might discover Dorothea's poetry tucked into her spare room drawer and get some pleasure from her lines. She hoped so.

She was just thinking about disturbing Oscar and venturing into the garden to look at the fence when the doorbell rang. Oscar sat up in her lap with a startled meow and leapt to the floor, giving her the eye as if it was entirely her fault. Which she supposed to him it was. With a reassuring smile, Dorothea stepped round him and made her way to the front door. Before she could get there, the bell rang again, this time more fiercely – if a bell could be fierce – and her mobile also started to ring.

Feeling rather brow-beaten at her sudden unaccountable popularity, Dorothea grabbed her phone to see who it was just as she opened the front door.

"Dorothea! Thank goodness you're in!" were the words that met her as she greeted her visitor. The next second, she was enveloped in a bear-hug that almost swept her off her feet. "I thought you'd never answer the bloody door. Or the bloody phone either."

It was her brother. What on earth was he doing here and at this time? As he crushed her to him, she could smell stale sweat and a faint hint of smoke. Regaining her footing, she pushed him gently away and stepped to one side so he could get in. Behind him, she couldn't see anyone else and swung round to confront him.

"Where's Leonora? What's happening?"

Bob's eyes darted round her hallway, looking anywhere but directly at her. "She's not here."

"What?" Dorothea stared at him. "Is it some kind of surprise? Where is she? It's her birthday! What on earth are you up to?"

There was a terrible silence. Bob's eyes finally met hers and he blinked. Then he blinked again. For the first time, Dorothea realised how pale and strained he looked.

"H-her birthday?"

"Yes," she replied, crisply. "It's your wife's fifty-fifth birthday today and you should be at home celebrating with her, and not visiting me for some unknown reason. *What in heaven's name is going on, Bob?*"

"Oh God, oh God, oh God," was her brother's only reply and he ran his hands through his hair, groaning. "Oh God."

Dorothea snorted in despair and put her hands on her hips. "You'd forgotten, hadn't you? You'd entirely forgotten about your wife's birthday and making Leonora's day a special one and instead you're here with me for reasons I can't even begin to understand! Did you have a row or something? Has she thrown you out?"

Bob looked up at her and there was something in his eyes that Dorothea couldn't read.

"Yes," he said. "Yes. She's thrown me out."

"Well, you must have done something foolish enough for Leonora to do that, mustn't you! Oh you stupid, stupid man. Come into the kitchen and I'll make you some tea – you look like you could use it. I'll ring Leonora and let her know that …"

"No!" Bob interrupted her as she started to key in the numbers on her mobile. "Don't ring Leonora! Please. Not yet, anyway. I'll ring her later, I promise. I just need some time to … to …"

"To what?" asked Dorothea.

"To think!" Bob finished his sentence with some force and then began nodding as if he was congratulating himself on his own idea.

"Yes. To think. I need to think, you see, Dotts. To make sure I don't make things worse, don't you see?"

Dorothea did see, sort of. Bob wasn't well known for his tact or his ability to make things better. Especially when she was sure that whatever had happened between her brother and Leonora would be Bob's fault. Perhaps he should wait until Leonora calmed down, though it was a crying shame this was happening at all, what with it being her friend's birthday. She also wished Bob wouldn't call her *Dotts* as it was a name only her girlfriends used, but she saw quite well this wasn't a battle to fight now.

"Well, all right," she said. "Come and have tea and you can tell me exactly what you've done to upset Leonora so much."

She turned and trotted into the kitchen, followed closely by her brother. Honestly, she wished he'd thought to have a shower before he fled here – the smell of him was making her wrinkle her nose and she opened the window before filling up the kettle again. From the corner of her eye, she saw Bob sit down and the next moment there was a fierce yowling as Oscar shot up from his position under the chair her brother had chosen and gave them both a furious glance.

"Oh God!" Bob said. "I'd forgotten about your bloody cat. He's never liked me."

"Don't call him names," Dorothea protested as she reached for a teabag. "His name is Oscar and you know it. Besides, you startled him with all your stomping about so you can't blame him for making his feelings known. There, there, Oscar, don't worry about the nasty man. I'm sure he's sorry for frightening you."

With that, Dorothea hunkered down and gave Oscar a quick stroke of his ears. He closed his eyes (how he loved his ears being stroked!), accepted her apology with a purr and then padded out of the kitchen to a place of greater safety, giving Bob a wide berth. She couldn't find it in herself to blame him.

She made Bob his tea in silence and then placed it in front of him. He nodded his thanks and took a sip.

"Sugar?" he asked. "Please?"

With the shock of her unexpected visitor, Dorothea had entirely forgotten about her brother's sweet tooth. She only kept sugar for him as nobody else who visited ever asked for it. She retrieved it from the cupboard and placed it next to him, with a teaspoon. She didn't bother with the sugar bowl.

Bob gave her a look and then sighed, probably realising he was lucky to get any sugar at all, no matter how it was presented. He took a spoonful, put it in and then added an extra half-teaspoon as well. He normally only had one sugar in his tea. Goodness, Dorothea thought, he must have *seriously* messed up in some way or other.

"When you've finished that," she said, folding her arms and giving her brother another hard stare, "you can go and have a shower because, honestly, you do smell a bit. Then you can come downstairs and tell me what on earth you've done. Agreed?"

Another short silence and then he nodded. "Okay."

"Good, in that case I'll let you drink your tea in peace."

Dorothea was at the kitchen door when he spoke again.

"Thanks, sis," he said quietly. "Just … thanks."

Without turning around, she nodded and then returned to the living room where she'd been sitting when Bob had arrived. Oscar was lying across her sofa, spreading his fur everywhere, no doubt. She eased him along until there was room for her as well and gave him a heartfelt cuddle.

"This is a surprise, isn't it?" she whispered. "What on earth is going on, do you think, Oscar?"

The only response was a gentle purr as she stroked him, so not much there to be getting on with. Hopefully, all would soon be revealed, and Dorothea could safely get back to the weekend she'd been planning. After a while, she heard the kitchen door shutting and the soft thump of footsteps going up her stairs. Then a few minutes later, the noise of the shower. Bob had taken her advice to heart, which could only be good news. At least he shouldn't be as smelly when he came back downstairs. It was just a shame she had no options for him to change his clothes, unless he'd bought some with him. But she couldn't see any set of circumstances when he would do that, if he'd left in a hurry. Whatever this turned out to be, Dorothea was sure it hadn't been pre-planned.

With a sigh, she eased herself away from Oscar who viewed her retreat with a wary eye, and made her way back into the kitchen. To her surprise, Bob had rinsed out his tea mug and placed it on the draining board. He must be feeling guilty for having suddenly arrived at her doorstep. She'd not known him tidy up after himself willingly before. Miracles could still happen, on occasion.

Dorothea busied herself downstairs until she heard the shower room door opening again.

"Have you eaten anything today?" she called upstairs.

"No, not yet," Bob replied as he came to the top of the stairs. He was drying his hair with a towel.

"Okay," she said. "I'll make you some toast and there's some cereal too, if you want it. While I'm doing that, you can use the hairdryer in my bedroom if you need to. It's on my dressing table."

"Thanks, Dotts," he said. "You're a star. Just toast is fine. I won't be long."

He was true to his word, and she'd only just taken the toast from the toaster when he walked back into the kitchen. His hair was already dry. Typical men, she thought. Their hair always dried in seconds whereas all the women she knew spent whole lifetimes drying their hair, no matter how short the cut.

"Jam or marmalade?" she asked as she put the toast rack on the table next to the plate and knives she'd already placed there. "The jam is strawberry."

"Jam, please."

Bob sat at the table as she took out the jam and pushed it across to him.

"Another drink?"

"Please. Coffee would be great, thanks."

She made coffee, and then pondered whether she herself would like one but decided against it.

When her brother began to eat his toast, she sat down opposite him.

"When are you going to tell me what's going on?" she asked.

He gave her a quick glance. "Soon. Really I will."

She nodded. She'd expected that. "And when can I ring Leonora to let her know you're here?"

"Again, soon. I promise you."

Dorothea pursed her lips. She wasn't satisfied with either of her brother's answers, but she knew quite well how further pushing on her part would only mean he'd clam up for longer. Still, her loyalties were torn between him and her friend, and she didn't like the unsettled feeling this gave her.

"Well," she said eventually. "It had better be sooner rather than later, or I'm definitely going to be ringing either Leonora or Selena to see what they might have to say about all this nonsense."

To that, there was no reply, so Dorothea left him to it and walked out into the garden to get some air. She needed it. To her surprise, Oscar followed her outside. He was usually more of an indoor cat than an outdoor one, though she never stopped him from going outside if he wanted to. He began to wind himself round her legs and purr, so she crouched down and smiled at him.

"Yes," she said. "Definitely better out here, isn't it? Goodness knows what's going on with my brother today, but he needs to sort himself out and get back to Leonora very soon, doesn't he?"

Oscar simply looked up at her and blinked. Solemnly she blinked back, and he continued with his purring.

Dorothea stood up carefully and made her way to her shed, with her cat not far behind. Taking her trug and putting her hammer and a box of nails into it, she walked across the garden to where her fence was most damaged. For the next hour or two, she busied herself making her boundary secure again. This area of the garden was always the worst for winter damage and she was undecided as to whether to change the entire fence. A possible job for the spring perhaps. For now, she was content with making do and mending – as her grandmother had used to say. The trouble with this part of the border was that the tiny stream behind it came closest to her land here and so her wooden fence suffered most, especially during winter. On the plus side, as the back of the border nearest the fence only tended to dry out fully in the height of summer, it was ideal for her astilbes which loved having their roots wet. There was a good side to every problem.

She was well into the fourth section of her fence-mending mission when her brother's voice behind her made her jump. She almost dropped the hammer.

"What are you doing sneaking up on me like that?" she said as she turned round. "I could have injured myself!"

"Sorry," he said, looking suitably chastened as he gestured back at the house. "It was just your mobile was ringing and I think it might have been Selena trying to get hold of you. Her name was on the screen when I looked at it. I wasn't prying or anything."

There was something about the way Bob was speaking that made the alarm bells in her head begin to sound. As she took a couple of steps towards him, he waved his arms as if trying to stop her returning indoors. *Just what the heck was wrong and why exactly had he turned up here today?* She was fed up with being put off and so her chin went up and she looked straight at him.

"Why is Selena ringing me?" she asked. "What on earth have you done, Bob?"

Once again, his gaze slid away from hers and he pushed one hand through his hair before starting to stutter something incomprehensible.

"Well, it's like this ... I mean it's been a difficult few months ... for both of us ... and ..."

"Oh, for heaven's sake!" Dorothea interrupted his ridiculous mumblings. "Why can't you come straight out and tell me what is going on? On Leonora's birthday of all days! Honestly, you never knowingly tell the truth when you think lies or silence will be easier. That's always been your way. And I have to tell you I don't like it. You might find your life is a lot more straightforward if you just *try to be honest once in a while.* Now, I'm going to check my phone and talk to Selena and don't even think about stopping me!"

With that, she sidestepped smartly round him as he stared at her open-mouthed and made her way equally smartly back inside her home. The expression on her brother's face amused her – she didn't usually raise her voice to anyone. She was glad she could still surprise him. He took her support and love too much for granted.

And of course she loved him – he was her brother. But he could be very annoying and ridiculous, and today was one of those days. She spotted her mobile where she'd left it on the living room table at once. As she hurried towards it, the ring tone started and when she picked it up, she saw it was Selena.

"Hello," she said. "Selena? It's me, Dorothea. Are you all right?"

"Yes! Thank goodness I've got hold of you," came the whispered reply and Dorothea had to concentrate to hear what her friend was saying. Which was utterly unlike Selena in every way as she could usually be heard from a couple of fields' distance. At least.

Then, as Dorothea continued to listen to what Selena was telling her, she forgot all about her friend's unusual quietness. This was due to the fact that Selena was at Leonora's house and didn't want her to overhear the phone call she was making. None of that mattered though, because as Dorothea heard what had happened, her grip on her mobile phone became tighter and the line of her mouth became ever more strained.

When Selena had finished speaking, Dorothea thanked her for letting her know what was happening, told her to give Leonora her love and she would ring them both as soon as she could. She'd wanted to go to see Leonora, of course she had, but Selena had strongly advised against it. Then Dorothea ended the call.

In the silence, she could sense Bob hovering behind her at the patio door, unable to come in or to leave, dithering like an idiot. She turned round to face him and, when she spoke, her voice was as low and intense as it had ever been.

"You stupid, *stupid* fool," she said.

Chapter Four

February

Leonora

Leonora was sitting in one of the local pubs near home waiting for her husband to turn up. A thousand thoughts were rushing through her head and she couldn't work out which she should focus on. They were all equally bad.

Because she had decided that today, Monday 7pm, after a particularly bloody day at the office, was a good time to see Bob for the first time since he'd left her. She had a very important question to ask him and one which would either change everything or nothing. More than anything, Leonora wanted to save her marriage, no matter what. And she was determined to do whatever it took to make that hope into a reality. She'd made a promise at her wedding ceremony and she was determined to keep it. Besides, she'd known and loved Bob for all her adult life, and she still felt the same way about him. What they had was worth fighting for. This terrible month was only a blip in their lives together, she told herself. Surely

Bob would come to his senses soon and everything would be as it should be once more. She had to believe that. She had to be strong.

However, if she'd known beforehand that work today would be such a nightmare, Leonora probably wouldn't have texted her husband last week. Mondays weren't usually this bad. She'd been unlucky. Which, she supposed, was nothing more or less than a continuation of her current run of bad luck. She'd thought about cancelling but, if she did, she wouldn't have the courage to ask to see him again. She'd only really done it in the first place as she'd drunk three-quarters of a bottle of wine and had come up with a plan. When Leonora first thought of it, she was utterly convinced it would work. She needed to take hold of the situation and not sit at home crying like a child each night, in between getting angry and wanting to punch things. She didn't want to live like that anymore. So she'd made her plans and asked Bob for a meeting. She'd thought somewhere neutral would be best, somewhere which didn't hold quite so many memories.

But now, as Leonora sat waiting at one of the window tables with a latte, she wasn't so sure. Maybe she should have asked him to meet with her at home – it was where he belonged, after all.

Blinking away ridiculous tears, she took another sip of her coffee and it was just at this moment that Bob walked into the pub. In spite of everything, in spite of what he'd done and how much he'd humiliated her, Leonora couldn't help the way her heart lifted at the sight of him. And, for an instant, it was as if they were back in the earlier, good times of their marriage – just two people meeting for a drink after work and wanting to be together. She didn't know where that feeling had gone.

He looked good, but different. As he glanced round the place and then spotted her, Leonora saw he wasn't wearing his usual suit. Of course he wasn't. Since she'd chucked him and That Woman out of the house, he'd not been back for anything, so he'd have had to buy a whole new set of clothes. She'd not thought about that. However, as he walked towards the table Leonora had picked, she could see he wasn't wearing the usual type of suit he went for either. It was a different cut entirely – Selena would have known what it was and who'd made it, no doubt – but even Leonora could tell it wasn't from Marks & Spencer. His hair looked different too. These unexpected changes made her gulp and set down her cup before she spilled it.

Half standing to greet Bob, Leonora didn't know if she should hug him or not. The decision was made for her when he reached out his hand and shook hers before easing into the chair opposite.

So that was it then. Just a handshake. He hadn't even bothered to smile. Leonora found herself blinking again but swallowed the feelings down. She couldn't afford to be derailed.

Before she could say anything, Bob shook his head. "Sorry. Forgot my manners. Did you want a refill of your coffee? Or something stronger?"

"No, thanks," she replied and would have said more but by then he was on his feet again and gesturing towards the bar.

"Okay, I'll just get a drink for myself then."

And with that, he was off, leaving behind a subtle cloud of aftershave that Leonora didn't recognise. How had so much changed in a month? The thought of it made her heart pound and her mouth feel dry. The plan she had for this hugely important meeting seemed to shimmer and start to fade even before it had properly started. But she wasn't going to give up now, just because things weren't going quite how she'd envisaged them. She needed to get a grip.

A few minutes later, Bob was back at the table and sitting down once more. He had a bottle of beer and a glass. Leonora refused to acknowledge the fact that he'd not bought any nuts or crisps for the two of them to share – it was what he used to do. When they were happy. But she wasn't going to make that into a Big Thing, or even comment on it. Not if she could help it. She took a breath to begin but her husband got there first.

"It's nice to see you, Leonora," he said, pushing his drink to one side and clutching his hands together as if to form a barrier between them. "I'm glad you asked to meet me and, once again, I'm really sorry about the way you found out about me and Belinda. It was the last thing I wanted to happen, believe me. So, what was it you wanted to say? I'll try to be as helpful as I can, I promise you."

To gather some kind of courage, Leonora gazed for several long moments around the pub. There wasn't a huge number of other people there – it was too early for serious drinkers and too late for the post shopping crowd. If such people even turned up on a Monday. It wasn't a popular going out kind of day, which was part of the reason Leonora had chosen it. Right now, the clientele, apart from Bob and herself, consisted of a group of teenage girls poorly dressed for winter weather and giggling over what looked to be a plate of chips (lucky them!) and an assortment of drinks; one lone man staring at his phone and muttering something under his breath at whatever he saw there; and an older woman with two young children who were giving their cokes and burgers their full attention. Their grandmother, perhaps. She looked tired, even from this distance, and Leonora's sympathies went out to her.

Putting all that to one side, Leonora turned back to Bob who was now sipping at his drink and frowning.

"Okay," she said, trying to remember the plans she'd been so excited about. "Okay, Bob. I know our marriage is in trouble at the moment and I know things are difficult. I also know we have a hell of a lot to talk through and a lot to come to terms with. Ever since … ever since *that night*, I've been angry and upset. And with good reason, but let's not get into that now. But the other thing I know – and it's the most important thing of all – is that our marriage matters to me. It matters to me more than anything. And I believe we're worth fighting for. I still love you, you see, and I want us to work on our marriage together, just the two of us. So I'm asking you to come home, Bob. To give up *that woman* and come home. Can we work on this together? Please?"

Leonora finished what she wanted to say and knew it hadn't come out in the way she'd practised, but it was the truth. She hoped it would be enough. She desperately wanted her husband home. She wanted that more than all the anger and pain he'd caused her. She wanted it more than anything. She *loved* him.

Bob said nothing. In all the scenarios Leonora had anticipated as to how he might respond, silence hadn't been an option. She stared at him, heart beating wildly. He was looking down at his beer as if it was deeply and entirely fascinating.

"Bob?..." she said, her hand reaching across the table towards his and then drawing back at the very last second. "Did you hear what I said?"

His head shot up as if she'd startled him or he'd forgotten she was there. "Yes! Sorry! I heard, yes. It was just you surprised me. I didn't think that's what you'd say at all. You've been so … so …"

"Angry," Leonora completed his sentence with a sigh, glad that the conversation seemed to be back on track, after a fashion. "Yes, I know. I've been furious. But can you blame me? Finding out you were having an affair was devastating. I can't even begin to tell you how awful it was. But that doesn't matter now – we can sort through all that kind of stuff. I *know* we can. We just need to give our marriage a chance. I know we're not perfect, but I'm as sure as I can ever be that we're worth saving. And I'm prepared to work hard at our marriage to save it, I promise you. Just as long as you're prepared to work hard too. Are you, Bob? Are you prepared to save our marriage?"

None of this speech had been in her plan. Even as Leonora was speaking, she realised how muddled and desperate she must sound. She'd intended to persuade him to come home where he belonged. She hadn't meant to put him on the spot like this.

"Oh Leonora," he said, patting her hand awkwardly. "That's really lovely of you. I know things have been difficult and I understand it's all been my fault. But …"

Oh. A *but*. Leonora might not have been in the most receptive of mental states, but she knew this wasn't a good sign.

"… But things between us haven't been great for a long while. Not if you think about it for a moment."

Hadn't they? What was Bob talking about? Yes, Leonora knew sex had been off the agenda for too long (and now she knew why), but they'd always got on well. They were friends as well as married. That's what she'd always thought. Leonora couldn't disagree with him more.

Her husband was still talking, however.

"I mean," he was saying. "We don't really have a lot to do with each other. Apart from being married and living in the same house. I'm not even sure we have a great deal in common – you have your life and I've got mine. We don't communicate well anymore. We've just been marking time, Leonora, rubbing along together. Is that enough to make a marriage worth saving?"

"What are you talking about?" she protested, a sudden rage filling her in such a way that it couldn't be denied. "There was absolutely nothing wrong with our marriage until *you* decided to have a bloody affair and bring the whole thing crashing down around our ears. So don't try to find excuses for your behaviour and don't even *think* about trying to put the blame on me. *Because I'm not the one at fault!*"

Without realising it, Leonora's voice had become louder and louder while she was speaking until by the end she was all but yelling across the table at her *bloody stupid* husband. When she stopped, the pub seemed for a moment to be utterly silent. Leonora saw the woman behind the bar staring at her and then immediately turning away when their eyes met and busying herself doing something with the optics. There was a slight snort from the group of teenage girls who were gazing at Leonora, their expressions rapt. Unlike the woman at the till, they just kept on staring, and it was she who turned away, her face bright red. The two young children had stopped eating and were also staring at her in open curiosity.

"Grandma! Why is that lady so cross and so red?" asked the smaller of them, a question which made the grandmother jump from her seat, gather up her charges and their assorted baggage and frogmarch them out of the pub and into the wintry street. All with a great deal of protest from the two children.

"Don't interfere, my darlings," she said with a lilting Welsh accent as she bustled them outside. "Why don't we go home and you can have some chocolate while we wait for your mummy?"

With that promise, they were gone like a shot, burgers and coke forgotten, thank goodness, though the taller of the two children was still staring at Leonora as they were hurried past the window.

Finally, and with a deep sigh, Leonora turned her attention to the man on his mobile phone to see how he might react to her unintended outburst. He wasn't looking at her at all but was instead still intent on whatever was going on with his phone. He probably hadn't even noticed. Typical bloody man! Lost in their own worlds and paying not a blind bit of attention to anything else.

"Keep your voice down, will you?" Bob whispered, leaning across the table. "I didn't agree to come here to talk with you just so that everyone else can know our business."

"Well, thank you so much for stating the ruddy obvious," Leonora whispered back. "And I hadn't realised it was such a pain for you to come here today."

"That's not what I meant and you know it."

"Do I? I'm not sure I know anything at the moment. You're just making up stuff about our marriage that's not helpful if we're going to try to work things out."

Bob didn't reply. He just looked at Leonora for a moment or two, and then took another sip of his beer.

"The thing is, Leonora," he said quietly. "I don't want to work things out. I'm actually happy with things the way they are."

Leonora blinked at him. His words were dancing in her brain like tiny fireworks and she couldn't grasp them for long enough to make a complete picture. Yes, she knew what they all meant separately but, together, they weren't making any sense.

"What do you mean?" Leonora said at last when she could speak again, at the same time trying with all her strength to keep calm. Then she played what she hoped would be her best card. "How can you be happy with things? You're not with *that woman* anymore. She chucked you out on the night you left. That's what Selena's told me. So what's going on?"

"Belinda," Bob replied, clutching his glass in front of him. "Her name's *Belinda*. And yes, she did chuck me out that night. Things were difficult for a while but we're back together now. And we're both happy about that."

"So what about us?" Leonora said before she realised she was even going to ask the question. "If you're so happy right now, what about me? Where do I fit in?"

"I don't know," Bob said, after a long and terrible moment. "I don't know, Leonora. I'm happy with the way things are for me, as I said. I honestly don't want to cause you any more pain beyond what I've already caused you, so I think we should leave this conversation where it is. Believe me, I'm very touched by how much you want to save our marriage. Please also believe me when I tell you how much you mean to me, but the way things are for me now are good and I don't want to change them. I'm sorry."

And with that, as Leonora tried to find the words to speak but couldn't, her husband patted her on the arm, got up and quietly left the pub.

His departure made her look like a total fool. She felt utterly humiliated and more confused than she'd been when he'd arrived. Far, far more.

Chapter Five

February

Selena

So far, the year had been pants, Selena thought, as she sat at the back of the very off-theatreland space she'd been invited to this afternoon. She wished she had someone to talk with about how all of it was affecting her friendship circle. But she couldn't chat with Leonora as it made her friend cry and she couldn't chat with Dorothea as … well … as bloody Bob was her brother and of course she would be on his side. That was natural. Selena didn't have to like it, but she understood it. She wished there was a way of getting Leonora to talk to Dorothea, but she wouldn't – or couldn't – right now, and Dorothea was far too nice to push for a conversation.

If it had been Selena who Leonora had been refusing to talk to, she would have travelled across whole continents and camped outside her good friend's door until she was absolutely forced to talk to her. But Dorothea was a very different character and would never dream of doing such a thing. If only there was a way of waving a magic time wand which would put everything back to what it had been, Selena would sell everything she had to possess it.

All these thoughts made a wild frenzy of colours scratch at her skin. In an attempt to refocus herself while she was waiting, she gazed round the would-be theatre to familiarise herself with the setting. Max had invited her here so she could discuss costume ideas with him and the set designer.

In all honesty, she'd been expecting something more *theatrical*, or even an actual theatre, especially as Max must be spending a lot of money and so would presumably want to have the best he could afford. This place, however, was little more than an old warehouse that used to belong to someone in Max's family and had been left to him a couple of years previously when that person – a distant cousin or aunt or someone – had died. He'd not done anything with it since then, apart from paying the UK agent every year to keep it in one piece.

The location was good – just on the edge of Islington where it bordered with Hackney, so quite a cool venue for an arty audience. The room where she was sitting was the largest space in the building and needed a clean – she could see the occasional clouds of dust drifting near the high-up windows when the light came in. There were other rooms too: a fair-sized office, a smaller kitchen area, and a pair of ladies' and gents' loos on the ground floor, plus a series of interconnected attic spaces on the upper floor. All this was what Max had explained to her as she'd not seen any of the other rooms yet. She was especially interested in the attic. It might be useful for props and costume storage. The last thing she wanted for her costumes was for them to be stored in a damp or dirty room. The colours and fabrics would never stand for it.

Still, in spite of her concerns, she could see why Max was keen to stage the play here. His costs would be kept to a minimum as he wouldn't have to pay for what he already owned. And if the room she was sitting in was properly cleaned and fitted out, it would make a decent setting. There was enough space for about two hundred chairs, she reckoned, and the lighting was good. The only issue was the lack of a stage, which might be a problem for putting on a play. Although she was no expert. Maybe they could build one. It shouldn't be too difficult for anyone remotely handy with a drill.

Selena was just starting to estimate how big the stage might need to be for the play and how that might cut into the seating space when

Max walked through the door from the kitchen and gave her a bright smile.

"You came!" he said. "I didn't know you were here."

When Selena had arrived twenty or so minutes ago, right on time as agreed, she'd rung the old-fashioned bell she'd found outside but nothing had happened. So she'd tried the door, which had been open, and had walked in to the main space Max had been telling her about in his many texts and emails. There she'd sat down to take in the feeling of the room. She hadn't realised Max was already here, though it might explain why the colours in her mind had been performing cartwheels since she'd arrived. She really should pay them more attention.

She smiled at him and repeated what she'd just been thinking. "I rang the bell but as there was no response I thought I'd come in and wait for you. I didn't know you were here."

"Ah," he said, grabbing a chair from alongside the wall and pulling it up to sit beside her. "The bell doesn't work, I'm afraid. It's on my long list of things to fix."

For a moment out of time, Selena didn't pay any attention to what Max was saying. She was far too focused on the way the red and gold auras danced around his hair, the way his smile made his eyes crinkle up, and the way his subtle and spicy aftershave was making her blood sing. Goodness, her hormones were kicking in big-time and she needed to get a serious grip.

"Sorry," she said when the silence seemed to be stretching out to eternity and beyond. "I wasn't listening. What did you say?"

He repeated himself with a laugh, and Selena nodded. "That would make sense though once your play's up and running, you might want to cover over the doorbell if you mend it. You don't want people ringing the bell and running away when you're in performance."

"True," Max said. "Does that happen a lot in this country?"

"Only when you least want it to," Selena replied, still unable to stop herself from smiling. What on earth was wrong with her mouth? "I went through a stage of doing exactly that to our neighbours when I was in my early teens."

"That figures! You strike me as a bit of a wild one. The kind of woman who carves her own path."

"Well, nobody else is going to carve it for me, so I may as well get on with it. Though back then I soon realised the neighbours weren't going to thank me so that phase didn't last long. And I promise not to be the person ringing your doorbell and running away now."

"Good," said Max. "That would be the last thing I'd want to happen."

Again, that strange silence between them.

"Anyway," Max spoke at last, thank goodness. "You've seen the main theatre space. What do you think?"

"It's good," she replied when she'd caught her breath again. "A good location and a good building, though it'll need cleaning up. And I was wondering what you were going to do about a stage."

"Yes, I'd wondered about that too," Max nodded, leaping to his feet and striding across the room as he talked. "I've decided not to have a stage, as such. My plan is to have the performance area at the end of the space where a stage would normally be, but also bring the actors into the middle of the audience for some key scenes to give a greater intimacy to the play. We'll leave room for exits and entrances, and I think the best area for that is between the audience and the office door. It's wider and easier than the cast having to go through the kitchen. And there's enough room in the old office for costume changes, if the actors each have their own areas. What do you think?"

His enthusiasm was infectious and Selena couldn't help but laugh. "You certainly seem to have it all worked out!"

"In theory," Max replied, walking back towards her now he'd finished gesticulating and explaining his plans. "But, as with all performances, the reality will be very different. Now, would you like to have the tour before our set designer arrives? He's due in about ten minutes and is always late so we have time."

Selena nodded and followed Max through into the office, watching how his colours danced above him. She'd expected to see a scattering of office furniture and possibly even some long-forgotten files, but instead the room was empty. Lit by a large window onto the outside space, it was filled with sunlight and dust in the same way that the main room had been, but with an entirely different set of colours.

"Oh," said Selena, spinning round and trying to take in the unexpected influx of pale cream, white and blue. "That's beautiful."

"What? What is?" Max turned round to stare at her, but of course he couldn't see what she could see. Nobody could. "It's just an office, Selena."

Yes, of course it was, but it was the colours that made it different. She wondered if whoever had worked here had been more creative than they'd been able to express – this was what the colours and their combination was making her think. Max was right in practical terms – it was an office, but she could see how he would have earmarked it for the actors' exits and entrances. And for costume changes too.

"But it's what you said," she replied after a moment or two. "It's perfect for your cast – it's big enough and so light and airy. You could easily put a small sofa along one wall for people to relax."

Max laughed, which once more made his eyes crinkle up in that very attractive way they had. "That may be true, but I don't need the cast to be relaxed – I need them to be on the alert for their entrance cues. They can relax after the show, not during it."

Selena nodded. His words made sense. However, the patterns the colours were making were full of peace and creativity and it would have been good to use them properly. She also thought that, no matter how alert the actors needed to be, it was always beneficial to be at peace. The two states weren't mutually exclusive.

Next, Max led her through to the kitchen which was much smaller than the office. In contrast, it was filled with depressingly grey and brown cupboards, as well as a sink, a kettle, a very old and tiny oven, and a microwave which looked new to her.

"That isn't original, surely?" she asked, pointing at the microwave.

"No, I added it in recently," Max replied. "The agent said the oven was unusable, so I thought it was the best thing to do. I'll need to put a *Do Not Use* notice on the oven for now, though if the play goes well and I stage another one here, I'll get everything replaced."

"Including the décor?"

"You mean you don't think the whole grey and brown look is a good one?" Max asked with a twinkle in his eye.

"That would be a very definite no. Thank goodness the kitchen isn't large enough for anyone to sit down in. Those colours would depress them in no time."

"Probably true. When I get round to redoing it, what colours do you suggest?"

The answer sprang to Selena's mind as if it had been there all along, just waiting to be spoken.

"Pale yellow and cream," she said. "*Very* pale yellow. It would make the room look larger and go perfectly with the colours in the office."

"There aren't any colours in the office," Max said after a second or two. "It's undecorated, though the walls are white, I suppose. But that's not really a colour."

Oh yes, it absolutely was. White was an almost perfect colour, and the basis of how everything blended together. You could never ignore white. But Max didn't understand that. He also had no idea about the colours she'd meant either, and it was impossible for her to explain it to him.

"But if you redecorated the office along the lines I was thinking, it would be cream, white and blue. The colours of the sea and sky. And they would blend in well with the new kitchen colours."

Phew, she'd covered that slip up well, she thought, though Max was even now giving her a quizzical glance. Not that she could blame him – she was usually far more careful about what she said about the colours she could see. There was just something about this man that made her more open. She'd have to watch herself in future. The last thing she wanted was for Max to think she was one colour short of a rainbow.

"Interesting," Max replied, his frown fading away. "I like your ideas, but I hadn't realised you were keen on interior design as well as fabrics and costumes. Still, I suppose an artist is always thinking in an artistic way."

Selena nodded. "Oh yes! I don't suppose it's something that can be helped. I imagine you look at things in a theatrical way as well. But you're right, I'll stop thinking about your rooms and start focusing on the costumes. Shall we see the attic as you said it might be good for costume storage?"

"Yes, of course," said Max, and turned towards a small door at the far end of the kitchen which Selena hadn't noticed. Mainly because Max had been standing in front of it.

Quickly, he opened the door, switched on a light inside and hurried up the stairs. She followed him, breathing in the scent of old dust and old dreams. When he stopped at the top, she bumped into him and apologised, even though the sudden contact had made his colours swirl round her for a moment or two and almost gather her up into their pattern before she found her balance again.

"S-sorry!" she said, though it was more of a squeak, much to her embarrassment.

"No problem," he replied before stepping out of her way.

The first attic room opened out before her. And Selena forgot about everything. Because nothing had prepared her for this. Of course she'd seen the photos of the place which Max had sent her and she'd looked at the map of the layout. But either Max wasn't great at taking pictures or the light had been terrible on the day he'd taken them, as what she saw in front of her was nothing more or less than a festival of sunlight flooding in from the dormer windows.

Selena had expected the series of rooms to be enclosed, but instead they were flowing from one to the other all the way to the end of the attic, marked only by an open arch at regular intervals. And there were shelves and cupboards, and long tables everywhere.

And the colours, oh the colours that were streaming along the rays of sunshine filling the room: soft reds and yellows, greens, lilacs, ivory and peach. She'd never expected this.

She turned to Max, who was looking at her with a mixture of amusement and curiosity.

"Wow," she said, which wasn't a word she used often, but it fitted the occasion so she was happy to use it again. "*Wow*. This is astonishing."

"Yes, it is, isn't it," Max agreed.

"Why is it like this?" Selena wondered out loud as she started to explore. "It's not like any other attic I've ever seen."

"That's true. They used to make fashion accessories here, back in the day, so needed light and space for the machines they couldn't fit in downstairs. The heavier machinery stayed on the ground floor, but they placed the smaller machines and all the items they were working on up here to keep them safe and clean."

Selena nodded at this, only half listening to his explanation as she continued to explore. The cupboards she opened were large enough to hang several costumes in, and the tables were perfect for working with fabric. Not only that, but the shelves were wide enough to store any amount of costume and fashion supplies and there was also plenty of space for fittings.

"It's perfect, absolutely perfect," she said when she finally arrived at the other end of the attic and swung round to view it all again. "It's giving me so many ideas for your play as well. I love it!"

Max laughed and started to reply but at that very moment, someone pounded up the attic stairs and she heard a loud shout: "Hello! Anyone there or are you burglars?"

Max rolled his eyes. "Ah, I think our set designer has arrived. Come and meet him."

The set designer must have been the tallest man Selena had ever met, well over six feet, taller than Max and towering over herself. When she shook hands with him there in the attic, she felt her fingers squeezed in the kind of firm grip that matched the man's height, even while she was blinking at the plethora of colours which surrounded him: gold and black and purple all offset with flashes of white. Definitely an artist but Selena had never met one with such an impassioned aura. His name was Grant Cobalt – which she was convinced wasn't his real name but which suited him.

As well as being the tallest man she'd ever met, Grant was probably one of the oldest she'd ever worked with as well. His first words to her – apart from announcing his name – were to tell her he was seventy-five years old this month and very happy *indeed* to be working with her on Max's *marvellous* play.

By the time Selena had thought to thank him, Grant was already several conversations ahead of her and had lamented the nightmares on the tube line, the lack of decent sandwich shops in London and how he hoped the dust in the theatre venue wouldn't trigger his allergies. From there, he eased into asking Max his vision for the play so he could start the set design and then asking Selena her thoughts on colours and fabrics. In fact, he only stopped talking when Max managed to get them both back downstairs into the kitchen, boil the kettle and thrust a mug of strong tea into Grant's eager hands. That done and a temporary silence achieved, Max poured another mug of tea for Selena and himself, and the three of them sat down at the kitchen table to think things through.

Whilst Grant took several swigs – which must have burnt his mouth but he didn't seem to notice – Selena caught Max's eye and they shared a smile. He raised an eyebrow as if to check with her that she was okay with Grant and his ebullience and she nodded back and smiled again. She'd already warmed to the talkative designer and could see how they could productively work together. Besides, when it came to business, she preferred someone who communicated well. There was nothing worse than people keeping their opinions to themselves as, if they did, she couldn't then tell whether her work was acceptable to them or not. That wouldn't be the case here.

With the tea finished, the three of them made their way to the main room once more.

"Ah," said Grant. "This is where you're putting on the play? I can't see any staging here though."

Max explained once more about his plans, and Grant pursed his lips, in the manner of a builder who suspected the job he was being shown would be more complicated than anticipated.

"But *Earnest* has quite a specific type of set," Grant replied. "Surely you're not thinking about doing minimalism for this one, are you?"

"No, perish the thought!" Max said. "My plan is to have the main set at the far end where you would put a stage if you had one, and then have some of the action coming out from there through the audience. The exits and entrances will be via the office so there won't be any seating near there."

Grant nodded and then stared round the room once more. "So the performance area is both at the end and through the middle of this space?"

"Yes," agreed Max.

"And there'll be a need for set design against that far wall, amongst the audience in some fashion, and also on the path from here to the office?"

"Yes, absolutely."

A broad smile passed across Grant's face, and he suddenly punched the air. "Yes!"

"Yes, what?" Max asked.

"Yes, I've always wanted to design a set for that kind of performance but never thought I'd get the chance. This is wonderful, thank you so much! I have so many brilliant ideas for this, you wouldn't believe it."

"That's great news," Max said. "But don't go mad and don't forget the budget. This isn't the West End."

"Oh, of course, of course. Trust me. Have I ever let you down?"

Max paused and frowned as if he were thinking seriously about this question. Then he smiled.

"No," he said. "No, you haven't."

Grant hugged him and then spent some time taking photos of the various spaces before declaring himself done.

"Lovely to meet you, Selena," he said. "And lovely to catch up with you too, Max. You're not in the UK often enough! I've seen what I need to see for the moment, so I'll go and draft a few ideas for you. I'll get those over to you as soon as possible. Must dash, my dears, things to do and people to meet!"

And, with that, Grant was gone, leaving behind him a whole tide of enthusiasm and a mass of gloriously swirling colours.

Selena couldn't help but laugh.

"What?" Max said. "What is it?"

"There's one thing I know already," Selena replied. "This project is certainly not going to be dull!"

Chapter Six

February

Dorothea

Dorothea was determined to deal with February in a more positive frame of mind. But it was proving to be a challenge. Since Bob and Leonora had split up, she'd tried everything to get her old friend to talk to her properly, but nothing had worked. Dorothea could understand why Leonora would assume her first loyalty was to her brother – and, in a way, she supposed it was. But loyalty, as in life itself, was a lot more complicated than one would assume.

Now, after a month of being polite in her attempts to get Leonora to talk with her, or at least to be in the same room, she'd decided to be a little more forceful.

This explained why she was bundled up to such an extent that nobody could see her face, and was sitting in their usual Covent Garden pub nursing a very small glass of white wine. It was 5pm on a chilly Friday night and she knew Selena and Leonora would be meeting here at 6pm without her. Well, that was what Leonora thought, but Selena had gone along with Dorothea's plan and had promised her she'd do her best to make sure Leonora stayed when she saw Dorothea.

She couldn't help feeling stupid. Already she'd received a couple of curious looks from the bar staff, at least one of whom would have recognised her easily if she hadn't been quite so wrapped up. She hoped she wouldn't be asked to leave. She also hoped Leonora would stay and give her a chance, but she couldn't be sure of it.

Dorothea took another sip of her wine. One thing she was glad of was there weren't too many people in the bar tonight. It was all so ridiculous that she should have to be skulking about like this, as if she and Leonora couldn't have a simple chat with one another and sort things out. More than anything, Dorothea wanted to reassure Leonora she would always be her friend, no matter how stupid her brother was or how many bad decisions he made.

And thinking of Bob, Dorothea understood there were other important decisions she would need to make in the very near future. When Bob had first left Leonora – or rather when Leonora had made him leave (and, in all honesty, good for her!) – he'd tried to break it off with Belinda but that had only lasted a couple of days before the two of them got back together. She'd hoped all this could have been sorted out by now but here she was, a month along from that awful day, and still nothing was resolved.

When she was younger, Dorothea had foolishly imagined that being in her fifties would mean life would be manageable. She'd never anticipated this type of problem. Not at all.

When she next glanced at her watch, she saw it was nearly 6pm. And when she went to sip more wine, her glass was empty. She glanced around the bar to see if her friends might have arrived, but they hadn't. She might just have time to get another wine then, which was good news. Because she didn't have the courage to confront Leonora on an empty glass. Tonight, even though she'd never been a serious drinker, Dorothea needed alcohol.

Hoping that her table wouldn't be taken whilst she was at the bar, Dorothea darted up to the counter, holding her empty glass. She was praying for a quick refill before getting back to her seat.

Just then, the pub door swung open and two very familiar women swept in. Selena was in the process of putting her phone in her bag, and Leonora was starting to unwrap a bright pink scarf from her neck. She glanced up and somehow, inexorably, her gaze caught

Dorothea's where she stood frozen at the bar counter, unable to move, unable to speak. Unable even to breathe.

Despite all Dorothea's efforts at disguising herself, Leonora recognised her immediately, as she stopped moving and the pub door clicked shut behind her. Selena continued to walk forward for a second or two until she realised Leonora was no longer beside her. She glanced back at her friend, then glanced forward again along the direction of Leonora's silent stare, and then she saw Dorothea.

"Oh," Selena said. "Oh bloody hell and shit. And what the hell are you *wearing*?"

The next moment, Leonora had turned on her heels, her glorious pink scarf trailing out behind her, and was walking away, out of the pub. Before Dorothea had even had half a chance to make peace with her.

And, suddenly, Dorothea had had enough of not being given that half-chance. *More than enough*. Abandoning her wine glass, the barman and Selena's confused disappointment without a second thought, she ran out of the bar and caught a glimpse of Leonora on the first step leading upwards to the main market. She flew after her, not bothering to shout as she assumed Leonora would pay her no attention. She pushed past the tables and chairs in the courtyard and reached the stairs just as Leonora was halfway up. From behind, she heard Selena yell out but she couldn't hear what she'd said. Didn't want to hear because she was *going to catch up with Leonora and make her listen if it was the last thing she did today*. She swore it.

At the top of the stairs, Leonora slipped. Taking any advantage she could get, Dorothea grabbed the pink scarf and twisted it round her hand so her friend couldn't get free.

Leonora was jerked backwards and stumbled against Dorothea but, due to the fact Dorothea was still pressing forwards to her goal, neither woman fell. Instead, they ended up in a tangle of scarf and hoods and coats at the top of the steps.

"Let me go!" yelled Leonora, trying to break free but there was no way on earth Dorothea was going to allow that.

"No!" Dorothea yelled back. "Not until you *listen to me!*"

And, to Dorothea's relief and perhaps because she so rarely shouted at anyone, Leonora stopped struggling. She turned round, blinked at Dorothea and began to cry.

Then the noise of running footsteps and someone panting up the stairs behind.

"Oh God," said Selena as she reached them. "You two! What are you bloody well like? Honestly, I wasn't planning on doing any running tonight. Not in these heels! Let's stop having a cat fight and come back to the bloody pub. *Please?*"

In Dorothea's grip, Leonora made a sound very much like a small and very angry dog growling and then finally shook herself free.

Much to Dorothea's surprise, as she thought she herself would be very much in the line of fire, her friend turned on Selena, eyes wide with fury.

"You knew," Leonora said. "You knew Dorothea would be here tonight, didn't you? That's why you were so super-keen to go out. All that stuff you said about celebrating how your new work project was going at the theatre and how very inspirational it all was – that was just nonsense. Nothing more than a trick to get me here and try to make me talk to Dorothea! *How devious and underhand can one woman get?*"

Dorothea cringed at the out-of-control fury in Leonora's face and words. More than anything, she hated confrontation. Perhaps she shouldn't have thought of this ridiculous plan, let alone tried to carry it out. It was a *really* stupid idea. Again to her surprise, Selena didn't burst into tears or try to placate Leonora in any way – though of course crying or attempting to appease anyone wasn't Selena's style. Instead, her gutsy friend straightened her shoulders and glared right back at Leonora.

"Yes! I agree," Selena said, her voice booming out so surely the whole of Covent Garden could hear it. "I'm absolutely the most devious and underhand woman in the whole wide world. I'm so very devious and underhand that I would do anything – anything at all, I tell you! – to get my two best friends to talk to each other again when there's no real need for them not to be talking in the first place! And if this terrible and totally appalling trick I've played on you doesn't work this time, Leonora, then I'll keep on thinking of other *even more terrible* tricks to get you talking to Dorothea again if it's the very last thing I do! *Do you understand?*"

When Selena finished talking, there was a moment of tense silence, even there in the middle of the busiest city in the whole of the busy world. Then a group of young people standing next to the line of shops opposite – who had been gripped by this unexpected and delightful drama happening in front of their eyes – began to clap and cheer.

"Yeah! You tell 'em, love!"

"Go for it, gal!"

"It's good to talk!"

The spell between the three women was broken at once, and Dorothea felt herself blush at the embarrassment of suddenly being a public spectacle like this. In an attempt to avoid further notice – though even she realised that particular ship might already have sailed – she tried in vain to burrow deeper into her layers of scarf and hat. Selena, of course, was in her element and, turning towards the cheering group, smiled broadly and gave them a slight bow.

"Always a pleasure!" she said, a reaction which only served to deepen Dorothea's discomfort. The evening wasn't going how she planned, not in any way. However, just as she'd resigned herself to going home with the haze of disappointment settled round her shoulders, Leonora gave a deep and heartfelt sigh.

"Oh, *all right*," her friend said. "I'll give the both of you fifteen minutes, but no more. And I'd better get a bloody large drink out of it for my pains."

With that, Leonora gathered up her pink scarf and wrapped it securely round her neck. Then, giving a slight smile towards Selena, she stepped down the staircase to the pub once more.

Behind her, Selena punched her fist in the air in silent triumph. Then, grabbing Dorothea's arm, the two of them trotted down in Leonora's wake. Dorothea felt a wave of relief wash over her, though her heart was still pounding. She couldn't believe she had a chance to make things right and was determined she'd do her best to save her friendship. But would a mere fifteen minutes be enough?

By the time they reached the pub moments later, Selena was in the lead and opening the door.

"Okay," she said. "Find a table for the three of us and I'll get a bottle in. Leonora – you're allowed half of the bottle, though we can always get another one if it's needed. And, Dorothea, for goodness sake, take those scarves and that hat off. You look like Nanook of the North and not in a good way. It's honestly not that cold."

Having given her commands, Selena hurried to the bar, leaving Dorothea and Leonora standing awkwardly together in the entrance. For a terrifying moment, Dorothea thought Leonora might make a run for it again, but instead she shook her head and glanced around the pub without looking at Dorothea.

"Did you get a table already?" Leonora said.

"Yes, yes, I d-did," was Dorothea's stammered reply. "It's over here."

Of course she had no way of knowing if her table was still free but, to her immense relief, it was, so she pulled out the nearest chair and gestured for Leonora to sit. Then she herself sat down in the chair opposite, leaving the space between them for Selena when she returned.

There was a terrible silence Dorothea knew she had to fill, simply because she couldn't bear it.

"I'm sorry," she said for what must surely be the millionth time, if only in her own heart, and somehow having the courage to look directly at Leonora. "For what my brother did. If I could go back and change things, if I could stop him being an utter fool, then I would. But I can't and I'm sorry. And whatever happens now, I want you to know I am one hundred percent your friend and I always will be. But please, please, Leonora, don't shut me out just because Bob is my brother."

Dorothea had at least another thousand things she wanted to say but she didn't know how to say them, so she stopped talking.

The silence came back but perhaps it was a tiny bit less terrible. How she hoped so, but she couldn't really tell. If she couldn't speak, and if Leonora wouldn't respond to her, then she had to do something. Desperately she searched her mind for what that something might be. Then, remembering Selena's suggestion, Dorothea began to unwrap herself from her enormous scarves and place them on the back of her chair. Then she took off her coat and added it to the scarves. Finally she removed her hat and patted down her hair. She felt like herself again. For whatever good that might do her. She wished Selena would hurry up with the wine as they definitely needed it. She was about to glance at the bar to check progress when Leonora spoke at last.

"The thing is," she whispered so Dorothea had to lean forward to hear what she was saying. "The thing is that I can't take any more lies or people deceiving me about things. Do you understand? Bob lied to me for months and now you lied to me as well about tonight. Or at least said nothing about it, which is worse. I can't take any more lies. *I just can't.*"

As Leonora finished speaking, the tears began to roll down her face. Dorothy got up at once, hunkered down next to Leonora and put her hand on her friend's arm.

"I don't know what to say," she said simply. "You're right. I'm so sorry about all the lies. It's terrible, but I just didn't know what to do."

Leonora was silent for another few moments and then wiped her eyes. She looked at Dorothea.

"Is this your version of a hug?" she asked.

Dorothea thought about this. "Yes, I suppose it is. I'm not a hugging type. But that doesn't mean to say I'm not your friend. I'll always be that. No matter what."

Leonora blinked. "Okay."

Dorothea wasn't sure what that might mean but there was no time to explore it. Because Selena came back at that very moment with a bottle of white and three glasses.

"I'm back!" Selena said needlessly. "And even more importantly I have the wine I promised."

With a quick glance between the two of them, Selena sat down and poured three generous glasses, while Dorothea returned to her seat. Selena then pushed two of the glasses towards her friends and took a firm hold of the third one.

"Right," she said, lifting her glass. "Before anything else happens, I'd like to propose a toast."

Dorothea clutched her glass, anxious to fit in, but Leonora shook her head.

"What possible reason could we have for toasting anything?" she asked fiercely. "My husband is cheating on me and doesn't want to come home, and my two best friends have clubbed together and lied to me to get me here tonight. So, as far as I can tell, I've got nothing to celebrate. And, by the way, your fifteen minutes is ticking away."

Dorothea gulped and took a swig of her wine, toast or no toast. She wondered once more what to say, but it was Selena who spoke.

"All those things are true, Leonora," she said. "And yes, what's happened to you has been shit. Utter and absolute shit. Nobody is disputing that, and both Dotts and I are sorrier about all of the shit than we can probably ever say. But, on the more hopeful side, you have two close friends who are desperate to help and support you in whatever you do, no matter who their relatives are, and they'll do anything to help you, as tonight must prove. So my toast is to good friends and what they mean to us."

With that, Selena raised her glass and gazed at Leonora. Leonora gazed back, frowning. Slowly and oh so carefully, Dorothea moved her glass so it hovered next to Selena's and waited. Whether several seconds or several lifetimes passed then, Dorothea could never afterwards say, but when at last Leonora took her glass and clinked it against the both of theirs, the relief was overwhelming.

By the time Dorothea had put her wine down, it was already half-empty and Selena's wasn't far behind. If Leonora stayed longer than the allotted fifteen minutes, it was going to be a two-bottle evening. At least.

Leonora's glass was, however, barely touched when she put it down on the table. There was still a long way to go.

"Okay," said Selena, breathing out a deep sigh and shutting her eyes for a moment. "Okay, thank you. That means more than you can know. Now, Leonora, I need you to talk to Dorothea. Because she's honestly not the enemy here."

If Dorothea thought Leonora might need more persuasion to say anything else beyond what she'd already said, she was soon proved wrong.

"All right," Leonora said, eyes darting between the other two women before looking down at her glass. "I've already said what I think to Dorothea about the deceit her family seem to like so much, and how I don't want any more of it. Ever. What more do you want me to say?"

"We do understand," said Selena, unexpectedly using the softest tones Dorothea had ever heard her friend use. "We truly do. Anyone in your terrible position would think the same. But the deceit Dorothea – and I – have been involved in tonight was because we love you, not because we don't. As I've already said in so many words and will keep on saying until you really see it. Unlike Bob, we want to be with you and support you. So there's a difference. A hugely important one."

Leonora looked up, eyes wide. She stared at Selena and then, for the first time that evening, she turned and looked at Dorothea. Really looked at her.

Dorothea blinked. Then she reached out and touched Leonora's arm.

"It's true," she said. "I'm your friend, Leonora, and always will be. I can't help who my family is. And, once again, I'm really, truly sorry."

Another silence and Dorothea wondered how on earth Leonora would react and whether this one meeting – here in the pub they all knew and loved so much – might be the end of this friendship she treasured. Then Leonora touched Dorothea's hand lightly where it lay on her sleeve and began to cry.

"I know," she said, between tears. "I know and I'm sorry too. For the way I've been acting this last month. It's just I didn't know what to do or say. Every time I thought of you, Dotts, and every time you tried to contact me, all I could think of was Bob, and I just got angrier and angrier and I couldn't cope. I'm so sorry."

With that, Leonora's tears turned to sobs and she covered her face with her hands and rested her head on the table.

"Oh honey," Selena said as she leant across and tried to hug as much of Leonora as she could. "It's so awful. I know, I know."

Dorothea couldn't reach her friend from where she sat, so she rose to her feet, feeling oh so much freer without the disguise she'd been wearing, and trotted round the table to hunker down next to Leonora once more. She put her hand on Leonora's shaking shoulders and began to murmur soothing words. Dorothea herself had no recent experience of relationships or breaking up with anyone so she didn't know what to say, but she hoped her tone of voice might be enough.

And it must have been as, after a few minutes, Leonora stopped crying and lifted her head from the table. She wiped her eyes and tried for a half-smile. Even though this didn't fool either of her friends, at least it was good she'd tried it.

"I need more wine," Leonora said. "I know I've not drunk much but I definitely need more."

"Good call," agreed Selena, but this time it was Dorothea who refilled their glasses and then decided to get another bottle.

As she approached the bar, the barman nodded at her and gave her a quirky smile. He wasn't one of the regular bar staff and was a lot older than the others. Dorothea assumed he must be fairly new, though she could vaguely remember seeing him here before a couple of times.

"Same again?" he asked her with a distinctive Australian twang to his voice before adding, "Is your friend okay?"

"Yes, thank you," Dorothea replied as she reached into her purse for her bank card.

"Yes to the wine or yes to your friend being okay?"

Dorothea handed over the card and nodded. "Both, I think. I hope. It's been a difficult month."

"Got ya. Glad you're all safely back inside though. I was a bit worried when you rushed out like that."

"Oh," said Dorothea, totally unused to such conversations with bar staff, or indeed anyone else she didn't know. "Yes, we're fine, thank you."

The barman nodded and pushed the card machine towards her as he grabbed the wine from the fridge behind him and opened it. Dorothea did the necessary with the finances and took the bottle with a polite smile.

"Thanks," she said.

"No problem!" he replied. "And if there's anything else you need, then please let me know."

"Okay," said Dorothea, feeling as if she had somehow been catapulted into uncharted but not necessarily dangerous waters. "We will. Thank you."

She returned to the table, faintly puzzled. Leonora was wiping her eyes but looking less as if she was going to explode or run out on them. As Dorothea sat down, she caught the end of the conversation they'd been having.

"Okay, yes, of course," she heard Leonora say and then Selena's reply, "That's so great, thank you.

"Here you are," Dorothea said as she put the wine on the table. "Is everything all right?"

"Yes," Leonora replied, her voice shaking but stronger than it had been. "As much as it can be. Selena and I were just agreeing that I'll stay. There isn't a fifteen minute rule. Not really. I'm not even sure there ever was. I'm sorry."

Once more, Dorothea felt a wave of relief wash over her. "Thank you. I've missed our conversations so much. I want to know how things are with you."

"I've missed them too," Leonora replied and took Dorothea's hand in hers for a moment before letting go again and fiddling with her wine glass stem. "Though I suppose you know how things are anyway from Bob, don't you?"

Dorothea shook her head. "Not really. Nothing more than the bare minimum. He doesn't tell me much. I think … I think he feels the same about me as you do. That if he says anything important to me, then it might divide my loyalties too much. But it's not like that, Leonora. I'll always be your friend."

Even as she spoke, Dorothea knew her words – though heartfelt – weren't entirely true, but that wasn't what mattered right now. What mattered tonight was to rebuild her relationship with Leonora. Anything else that needed to be faced up to later would have to wait.

For the rest of the evening, the three women caught up with each other in a way they hadn't been able to since that January night. It meant the world to Dorothea, and the anxiety she'd been holding onto for the whole month eased its grip on her just a little. Because of this, she found herself better able to concentrate on her two friends as she listened. Leonora of course was the one she was most concerned about. As Dorothea learnt how her month had been since she'd split up with Bob, she found herself getting angrier and angrier with her brother and the way he was dealing with this. Or not dealing with it. In her view, he wasn't giving Leonora half a chance to try to cope with her marriage breakdown. As far as she could tell, Leonora had been very open indeed about what she wanted to happen, which was the mending of her marriage – far more open than Dorothea would ever have been. She didn't think she'd have had the courage to meet Bob as Leonora had done and ask him to come back to her. And Bob should have responded in kind to that offer, in Dorothea's view, but he hadn't. He'd just said something even more hurtful and left Leonora to deal with the aftermath. Again.

Right now, Leonora was looking as pale as Dorothea had ever seen her, and the bags under her eyes were a tell-tale sign of her exhaustion. Dorothea wished everything might be as it should be again, but it couldn't. That kind of fantasy was for children, not the adults they were. She and Selena would just have to do all they could to help Leonora through this. Somehow.

And, talking of Selena, she looked even more glamorous than usual tonight. Her hair was shining in the overhead lights, and she was wearing one of those striking outfits she loved so much. Her dress was deep blue and sparkly, and matched with a bright orange chiffon scarf and shoes. Her coat was one Dorothea hadn't seen before and suited her clothes perfectly, being blue with orange buttons. The whole ensemble was finished off with gold earrings shaped like tiny harps. Dorothea couldn't help but smile to herself and wonder how she'd managed to find a friend so very different in every way from herself. There was more than that, however. In a strange way, Selena seemed to shimmer, as if she had an aura around her which was making her glow. It must be a trick of the light, but that was how it looked. All very odd.

When Leonora had reached the end of the story of how she'd been doing recently, she seemed more than happy to sit and listen to what had been happening in Selena's life. It was almost the same as how they'd used to be together, a thought which made Dorothea's eyes well up, though she was wise enough to blink the tears away.

And Selena appeared to have had quite a month. There was the new play she had to create the costumes for, and therefore a new producer to get to grips with, and a brand-new venue too. All this sounded like a great deal of hard work to Dorothea.

The strangeness of other people and their lives was a constant mystery, but at least Selena seemed very excited by it all. In fact every time she mentioned the name of this producer – Max – her glow seemed to deepen a little more.

Just as Dorothea was wondering if it would be a good thing to ask the barman for a jug of water as well as the wine they'd ordered, the man himself appeared at their table. Almost as if she'd conjured him out of nowhere, and she couldn't help but jump a little when she saw him. So much so that she spilt some of her wine over her hand.

At once, the man grabbed his cloth and patted her dry.

"So sorry," he said, his accent drifting over the table like a small but soothing river. "Didn't meant to startle you ladies. I just wondered if I can clear the table for you and if you needed anything else?"

"Yes, that would be lovely," Selena said with a smile, her eyes darting between the barman and Dorothea.

Embarrassingly, the barman was still patting at her hand. So Dorothea eased her fingers away whilst nodding her thanks in his direction.

"We're probably all right for wine," Selena continued. "But how does everyone feel about grabbing a snack here rather than going to one of our usual places for food?"

Leonora nodded. "Yes, that sounds good. Not sure I'm up for much eating tonight, but a snack would probably be wise."

Dorothea could only agree, so they decided on a couple of chicken burgers, a plate of chips and a small green salad to share. The barman hurried away to get their order.

Selena leaned in.

"Nice arms," she said and then, "I think he *likes you*, Dotts."

Dorothea rolled her eyes. "Oh for goodness sake, don't talk nonsense. He's at least ten years younger than me and he's just being a good barman, that's all. Anyway, I don't think now is the time. We don't want to talk about men, do we? Not even in fun."

She desperately wanted to spare Leonora any unnecessary pain and was annoyed at Selena for even thinking of such things, let alone saying them. But Leonora surprised her by shaking her head.

"It's fine," her friend said. "I don't mind. I'd like to focus on something that isn't as disastrous as my marriage. So if you can find the right man for Dotts, then I'm all for it."

There was a silence as Dorothea tried to take in what Leonora had just said, but then her two friends burst into laughter. Dorothea sighed. Deeply. And took a sip of her wine.

"Sorry," Selena said when she'd finished laughing but actually not looking sorry at all. Not even remotely. "The look on your face! Priceless. Absolutely priceless."

Dorothea was more than sure she was right about that. She left relationships to other people. She much preferred a quiet life.

The rest of the evening was far more enjoyable than Dorothea had expected, in spite of the shadow hanging over Leonora. It was nice to get together with her friends again and remind herself that she did indeed have a life beyond work and commuting and gardening. And caring for her beloved Oscar of course. She was so glad Leonora had decided not to cut her out of her life after all. That would have been unthinkable.

When the evening was done, the three of them agreed to meet up sooner than usual to have a proper meal together. So Dorothea made her long way home with a far lighter heart.

By dint of running like an anxious hare across the station concourse, she made it onto her train just before the doors were shut.

This was more good news as, if she'd missed it, she'd have had another forty-five minutes to wait before the next convenient train. Choosing a carriage with as few people in it as possible, she settled herself into a corner seat. She placed her coat, hat and scarves on the seat next to her so she could be sure of remaining on her own until she got home.

Then, retrieving her mobile from her handbag, she texted her usual taxi firm asking for a lift from her station. They were well aware of her monthly Friday schedule. A couple of minutes later and she'd received the acknowledgement. That set her mind at rest. It was perfectly possible to walk home but she didn't want to do that at this time of night. Where she lived wasn't a dangerous part of the country, but she liked to be careful.

That all sorted out, Dorothea sat back and closed her eyes. She never slept on trains, ever, but she did like to think. And now, there were two main thoughts in her head she had to ponder over.

The first was a good one: how happy she was about the way tonight had gone, in the end. Though perhaps she could have done without the mad rush across the pub courtyard and up those stairs in order to stop Leonora from escaping. She was sure she hadn't run that fast for anything since the 1970s. At least. That particular dash had been for a bus to take her to do some last-minute Christmas shopping if her memory served her correctly. Happy days. Her parents had been alive back then and today, so many years on, she still missed them. She wondered what they would have thought of what Bob had done. They would have been horrified, she knew. And rightly so.

Remembering these things brought her full circle round to thinking about Leonora and Bob again. Dorothea's heart ached for Leonora, and for her brother too, but in a very different way. Once more she wished Bob had never met Belinda and that everything could be as it was surely supposed to be: Leonora and Bob still together; Selena being her mad and unique self; and she herself getting on with her life and enjoying being part of their friendship circle.

Now, everything had changed. Over the next few months, there would be so many decisions that needed to be faced, and so many unwelcome conversations to be had, that Dorothea could hardly bear to think of them. Perhaps she should simply live in this moment and let the future do what it had to. It usually did.

Her second main consideration as the train rumbled along bringing her ever closer to home was more personal. Because the thoughts drifting round her mind were very much to do with the barman who'd served them tonight and also to do with the reaction of her friends. Selena and Leonora had teased her about the man. Which was stupid as nothing would happen and she didn't want it to. Dorothea lived a single life and was more than happy with it. She had no desire to change and, besides, the barman certainly didn't *like* her in the way Selena had teased. Perish the thought. He was just being a good barman, that was all.

No, what made her heart sore wasn't any of that. What made her heart sore was the very fact of the teasing, and what it had meant, harmless though it had been. Selena and Leonora were her friends and would never knowingly hurt her. She knew this, of course she did.

But the question at the heart of their teasing and the one that was puzzling her so much was this: was she so very unlikely to ever be in a relationship at all?

Chapter Seven

March

Leonora

Today was the day. The first Saturday in March. Leonora woke up at 7am. This was earlier than usual for the weekend but the sun was peeking through the top of the curtain and must have caught her eye. For one glorious moment, her mind was blank, but then everything came flooding back.

She stared up at the ceiling, tracing the thin crack that had been there since forever and which had never got any bigger so it was nothing to worry about. Just the house settling into its true foundations. Or that's what the builder had told them. She remembered liking the whole concept of something settling into its true foundations and she'd thought, back then, that she had such foundations in her life already, but it had turned out to be a lie. Leonora's foundation had been her marriage to Bob, and now it was as if she was spinning in a void somewhere with no hope of a safe landing.

Rubbing her eyes, she told herself not to be so bloody ridiculous and got up. There was no point staying in bed, even for another few minutes. She needed to do something, if only to stop herself thinking.

Bob would be here at 11am and Leonora had promised to be ready for him. In some fashion or other. She'd been preparing for a couple of days already so she knew it wouldn't take long to get things organised this morning. What she didn't know – and couldn't begin to decide – was whether she herself would be here or not when he arrived. She'd gone over and over it in her head and had come to a different conclusion each time. She would have to make a final decision soon.

By the time she'd had a bath and eaten breakfast, she had a headache she wasn't sure she could shift. It was the sort of headache she used to have when she was in her teens and twenties, and she was half afraid it might turn out to be a migraine. Which was the last thing she needed today.

Once Leonora had set the dishwasher to begin its cycle – so few dishes in there these days – she stared for a long moment through the kitchen window, briefly admiring the way the sunshine sparkled through the early daffodils dotted through the neighbour's front garden. Nature simply carried on. No matter what else was happening.

Glancing at her watch, Leonora saw it was coming up to 8.30am. There was plenty of time still to decide what she would do. As long as she made a decision by 10.30am, it would be all right. So she made her way upstairs to the main bathroom, brushed her teeth, put foundation and powder on her face, tied back her hair and set to work.

She walked slowly downstairs and into the living room. Then, with a sigh, she picked up the large cardboard box she'd left there last night and moved it into the hallway. It took a while as it was heavy. In the end, rather than do herself an injury carrying it, she resorted to pushing it across the carpet and into the hallway, finally coming to a stop when it was near the front door. She supposed there was no need to be surprised at the weight – there was a lot in there, including the mugs she'd bought Bob for Christmas five years ago and which he'd never opened. They boasted a set of funny work sayings Leonora had thought he'd find amusing. She'd thought he might even take them to his office, but the mugs had been put in the back of a kitchen cupboard in the New Year and hadn't seen the light of day since. Well, he could jolly well take them with him now when he turned up. She didn't want them in the house anymore. Not even in that cupboard where she couldn't see them.

There were other items in the box too: a paperweight from Bob's old university, his set of Dickens novels and an old toolbox she'd found in the garage. No wonder it had been heavy! It was amazing she'd managed to lift it in the first place. No doubt she'd have an aching back tomorrow for her pains.

Leonora turned away from the box and went upstairs once more. In the bathroom, she opened the cabinet and began systematically to remove all the items belonging to her husband: his shaver, his electric toothbrush, two deodorant aerosols and three bottles of aftershave. She took these through to the bedroom and placed them carefully on the remaining space on the bed.

After that, Leonora went through the spare bedrooms to see if there was anything else that might belong to Bob though she couldn't exactly think what these might be. He tended to keep his belongings fairly contained and the spare rooms had mostly been her domain. They held more of her books and the old records she'd had when she was a teenager. Not that she could play them as she didn't have a record player, but they were part of her history and she couldn't throw them away.

Bob didn't feel the same; she was *his* history but he'd not paid her any heed when he'd started his affair. Perhaps he'd always had the gift of cutting himself off from his past when he started something new, but Leonora didn't have that skill.

There was nothing she could find in the upstairs rooms this morning that she hadn't already added to the boxes on the main bed. She should bring them downstairs now, but she didn't have the heart for it. When Bob arrived, he would have to collect them himself. But did she want him to go upstairs? This was where Leonora had last seen him in the house, on the bed with that woman. She squeezed her eyes shut to try to get rid of that terrible image, but it was harder than she thought.

Because of all this and because of the rising tide of grief which were making itself known in a way she couldn't begin to handle, Leonora went downstairs, put the kettle on and made herself the strongest coffee she could manage. This she took into the living room, along with a packet of dark chocolate digestives she'd treated herself to last week but not yet opened, and sat down. She didn't choose her usual place on the sofa, but instead sat on one of the two single seats which were part of the original suite. She took a sip of coffee, closed her eyes and attempted to think of nothing.

This didn't work. There was too much going on in Leonora's life. Besides, thinking of nothing had never been a skill she'd been good at. And it was even more hopeless to try it today. Because all she could remember was the first time she met Bob.

Leonora had been in the second term of the business secretarial course where she'd met Selena and Dorothea. So they'd only known each other about three months or so. However, by then, Leonora had known everything about Selena there possibly was to know, but virtually nothing about Dorothea. Perhaps Leonora should have been warned by that, but the problems she was having now weren't anything to do with Dorothea. Once Leonora had finally agreed to talk with her last month at the pub, she'd seen how ridiculous she was being. Dotts was her friend and always would be, whereas Bob was her bloody husband and didn't want to be. That was the difference.

But when Leonora had met Bob that first time three months after Selena and Dotts and she had become friends, it was as if she'd turned a corner where she'd been scrabbling around in the dark and had suddenly seen an unexpected shaft of light that made everything around her and inside her softer and more beautiful. Yes, she knew how over-the-top this sounded and how unlikely, but it was the nearest thing to the truth she could find. Their meeting hadn't even been planned. Bob and his mates had happened to be in the same bar the three women were in, and he'd popped over to say hello to Dorothea. Of course, Dotts had introduced him. When Leonora first turned to look at him and shake his hand, it was as if everything changed for her. Though, looking back, she didn't think it had been the same for him. Leonora was just a friend of his sister. Nobody special.

From the very beginning, Bob had always been special for her. There in that dingy old pub, something vital had altered in her bones and she couldn't do anything about it. Not then and not now. Leonora didn't even remember what Bob had said in the five minutes of chat he shared with them before returning to his own friends. It couldn't have been anything witty or profound but it didn't need to be. Bob could quite honestly have recited his shopping list and Leonora would still have been starry-eyed.

Once he'd gone back to his own group, she spent the rest of that evening downing lagers and desperately trying to get information about Bob from Dorothea. How old was he? Did he have a girlfriend? Did he even like girls? What did he do? What sort of things did he like doing? And most important of all these many, many questions Leonora bombarded poor Dorothea with: *do you think he liked me?*

Impossible of course for Dorothea to know the answer to that last and vital question. But at least she could answer the practical stuff – albeit reluctantly and with several vain attempts to change the conversation topic. Bob was two years younger and therefore the baby of the family, she told Leonora. Yes, he liked girls and had split up with his girlfriend about a couple of months earlier and, no, there was no chance of them getting back together again (Leonora asked this at least five times), because the girlfriend had gone off with someone else and hadn't been that into Bob in the first place. She must have been mad, in Leonora's view. He was currently starting an engineering apprenticeship and was getting really stuck into it. And he was a keen fan of rugby.

All the time this was going on, Selena was laughing and making kissing faces when she thought Leonora couldn't see. She was keen for Leonora to go over to Bob and ask him out there and then, but the very idea horrified Dorothea (and Leonora) so much that eventually Selena took pity on them both and stopped her teasing.

That night, Leonora dreamt of Bob and was utterly convinced they'd get their happy ending. She just had to make sure he noticed her. And for the next month or two, this was exactly what Leonora did. She followed him round as much as she could, even turning up at a couple of his rugby matches on a Saturday afternoon, when, really, she would have been much more in her comfort zone either shopping or lazing at home. It was hard to know what on earth was going on as the match was played, but she kept an eye on everyone else and cheered when they cheered and groaned when they did. She hoped it would be enough.

And, astonishingly, it was. Though Leonora suspected that, in these modern days, her obsession with her friend's younger brother might have been bordering on stalking, but back then they were ignorant of such things. In any case, it worked and, about two weeks after she'd struggled through yet another rugby match, Leonora had a phone call from the man filling her dreams night and day.

She almost didn't answer. It was only because her mother picked the phone up just before the answering machine clicked in that Leonora got to take Bob's call at all. As she was sure that Bob would never have bothered leaving a message. Boys didn't do that. Not then and not now. If they bothered to communicate in the first place. She must have sounded like an idiot on the phone, giggling like a child and not able to form proper words but it was like all her wildest dreams coming true at once. So she couldn't think properly, let alone find something sensible to say.

By the time Leonora got off the phone, her mother was hysterical with laughter and expressed her utter relief that the man her daughter had been talking about non-stop for weeks had finally asked her out. Leonora hadn't thought she'd been that obvious, but was far too happy to argue her case. In fact, she remembered grabbing her mother's hands and the two of them dancing round the kitchen table and almost breaking the teapot. Not something she ever admitted to Bob, or indeed to her two friends.

On that first date, which took place three days after he'd phoned her (and what a long three days they were), Bob and Leonora went to the pub for a couple of beers and some extremely hot chips – so hot that Leonora nearly burned her mouth. Afterwards, they walked slowly into town and wandered with no particular purpose along the high street staring at the shop windows and laughing at the prices. Frankly, she wouldn't have minded what they did just as long as they were together. She didn't remember what they talked about. What she did remember was their first kiss at the end of the evening and how magical it felt. As if everything afterwards would be utterly different from her ordinary life, and touched with gold.

After that, they became an item until Bob went off to university. To Wales to study Engineering. A million miles away as far as Leonora was concerned. She would have done anything to keep him as her boyfriend but he was determined that a long-distance relationship wasn't fair on either of them. And so, when he left to start his new life, Leonora was devastated, though she tried hard not to let him see it. Girls were never allowed to show boys how they really felt. It's what all the magazines told them.

So it was Selena and Dotts who suffered the fall-out when Bob and Leonora parted. Much as they were suffering now, she supposed. Back then, with Bob away studying and no longer her boyfriend, Leonora spent long days and nights weeping and wishing with all her heart that things could have been different. Dotts and Selena spent so much time with her then, either together or on their own. She didn't remember much of what they said, apart from one night when Dotts and Leonora were sitting on Leonora's bed in her new shared flat, eating their way through an enormous bar of chocolate and watching crap television. Leonora was sobbing gently when Dotts shuffled along on the bed and put one hand on her arm.

"Leonora?"

Leonora turned towards her, her mouth full of chocolate and her eyes full of unshed tears.

"I know you're really unhappy now," Dotts said quietly. "And I'm sorry. But, you know, even if it might be the end of this particular chapter with my brother, it might not be the end of the whole book. Just thought I'd say that. In case it helps."

For a long moment, Leonora stopped chewing her chocolate and felt the comforting warmth of it in her mouth. Even the television seemed to be quieter. She didn't really understand what her friend had said but it might have been the wisest thing she'd ever heard, then and now.

Back then, Leonora broke the moment and nodded. "Okay. Thanks."

Dotts was right too, though it took a long time, or what seemed to be a long time. Because six months after Bob gained his 2:1 degree, he returned to his home town after travelling across Europe, and started working. Two months after that, he and Leonora were an item once more. And the rest, as people say, was history.

Until now. When Leonora opened her eyes in her lonely house, she was still facing the break-up of her marriage. And, when she looked at the clock, it was somehow ten minutes to eleven and Bob would be arriving any minute. She wasn't ready. She would never be ready. She didn't know what to do.

Leaping up, Leonora ran down the hallway and to the front door. She was going to leave before he got here – the decision had been made without her knowing it. She should have realised how simple it was. She didn't want to see him, she just couldn't face it.

Then she ran back to the hall cupboard and grabbed the first coat she found there. But as she retraced her steps to the front door, heart pounding with the utter and overwhelming desperation *to be gone*, Leonora was already too late. She could see the outline of a man – Bob – behind the obscured glass panel, and the ring of the doorbell pierced the air. Stupidly, she took two steps back and felt the banister jabbing into her back. As if she could stop him coming in and prevent this next terrible stage of their lives happening, but of course she couldn't. Bob had a key. He was just ringing the bell to check if she was there. That was all.

Taking a deep breath, Leonora tried to find what little courage she had, and went to open the door. Bob half-jumped as if he hadn't expected her to be there, and for that she couldn't blame him.

"Oh," he said. "I didn't think … Anyway. Are you on the way out?"

Leonora stared at him and then realised she still had her coat on. Looking down, she saw it was the coat she used to mess around in the garden. Bob should have known it had never been her going-out coat. It was far too shabby. Though he'd never paid any attention to that kind of thing.

"Oh, no!" she replied, stepping back and allowing him to come in. "I mean, it's my garden coat. I've just … come back in from there. Do you want a drink?"

"No thanks," he said, eyes darting around at everything apart from her. "I'm here to pick up the rest of my stuff, as we agreed."

"Yes. Okay. I've put what I could find in boxes," Leonora waved one hand at the pile of boxes further down the hallway. "But there are still some things upstairs. In the bedroom. You'll probably want to have a look at those. Take what you need."

She shut up. She was burbling like an idiot and felt the tears pricking her eyes once more. She had no idea how some women dealt with this kind of thing with dignity.

"Thanks!" Bob said with a display of false enthusiasm that sounded utterly unlike the husband Leonora thought she knew. "I'll get to it then!"

Without looking back, he trotted upstairs and a moment later she heard his footsteps in the bedroom overhead. Looking up at the ceiling, she wondered what he was thinking, what he was doing. She wondered also at how empty the house – and her life – would become when he was finally and completely gone.

A silence and then she heard his footsteps coming out of the bedroom onto the landing.

"Leonora? Is it okay if I take a quick look around up here to see if there's anything else? I won't take anything of yours, I promise."

Shutting her eyes briefly, Leonora nodded before realising that of course he couldn't see her from where he was standing. "Yes, sure, go ahead."

She'd tried to sound as upbeat as he was being, but didn't think her voice was convincing. Not sure she could say anything else without bursting into tears, Leonora shut up and headed for the kitchen. There, she sat down on the nearest chair and put her head in her hands, trying to breathe deeply and calmly. At least that headache she'd been worrying about earlier on seemed to have eased, which was a blessing. But she felt sick to the stomach instead, which wasn't much better.

From upstairs she heard Bob moving about the rooms, checking if there was anything else left to take. That it had come to this! All their years together, all the love she'd given him, all the love she'd thought they'd shared. Where did it go and how had she lost it? *Why had Bob had an affair with that woman?* And how could she not have realised what was going on? Leonora had never felt so hopeless in her whole life. There must be something she could do – something that would even now convince him to stay, to give *them* another chance – but she couldn't think what that magic solution might be. She'd already tried with all the words she knew in the pub, and he'd walked away. There was nothing else to say now.

How Leonora wished she'd left before he arrived. She didn't have the strength to bear her husband walking away from her. It was a slow torture, having him in the house like this.

She didn't know how long Bob remained upstairs but at last Leonora heard his footsteps coming down again. His tread sounded heavier. Brushing her hair back from her face, she got to her feet and walked slowly into the hallway. Her estranged husband was making his way down the stairs, carrying one of the boxes she'd put out on the bed. She could see the tip of his hairbrush peeking out from one corner with a couple of shirts next to it.

The sight of them made her stomach twist again, but Leonora tried somehow to smile. As if all this was going to plan. Whatever that plan might have been.

"Thanks for getting everything together for me, Leonora," he said, again in that very upbeat tone of voice. "You didn't have to do that."

She didn't reply. Yes, she supposed he was right and she hadn't needed to do it. But the thought of Bob being in the house where they'd been so happy – or so Leonora had thought – for longer than necessary had been too hard to cope with. She'd anticipated that it would be better for him to be in and out of the house in as short a time as possible but, now he was here, she didn't want him to go.

"I'll start putting all this in the car and then I'll be off. Though if you do find anything else I might have missed, could you let me know?"

He gave Leonora a sideways glance and she nodded. She still found herself unable to speak. He began to carry the box he was holding to the front door.

"Sorry," he said. "Could you?..."

For a moment, Leonora didn't know what he was asking and then she realised. She rushed to the front door, brushing against him in the hallway as she sped past. She opened the door and he shuffled through, refusing even to look at her.

"Thanks," he said as he stepped outside. "I'll be back in a minute for the others."

There was something about this slow leaving that Leonora couldn't handle anymore so she left the door on the latch and went back to the kitchen. She didn't want to watch Bob taking his belongings away. She couldn't do it. Because her legs were trembling, she had to sit down. Something inside her felt blank and so very empty that she didn't know how she could ever fill it again.

She heard Bob come in and out, up and down the stairs a few times, and then after a while there was nothing. She strained her ears to hear what might be going on, but there was only silence.

Then, from outside, the sound of a car starting. Leonora jumped up, unable to believe it, and ran to the kitchen window. There, she saw Bob's silver Toyota backing out of their driveway and into the main road. *The bastard.* He'd bloody left without letting her know he was going and without even saying goodbye. How dare he! From being torn with grief and loss, Leonora was thrown into the kind of rage she'd never experienced before. Something black and scarlet and burning out of control. Worse than her fury at discovering him with *that woman* in her bedroom on that January night.

Leonora ran from the kitchen into the deserted hallway and flung open the front door which was still on the latch.

"You bastard!" she yelled at the departing car, her whole body shaking with fury. "You *utter despicable cowardly bastard!*"

Her voice rang out across the street and she saw one or two curtains twitching, but she didn't care. Reaching down, Leonora picked up the nearest thing she could find, which was a pot full of spring bulbs she'd bought to cheer herself up only last week. Then she ran halfway down the drive and flung it with all the strength she could muster at Bob's car as it began to drive away. Astonishingly it hit the wing mirror and bounced off into the road.

"That'll show you, *you bloody bugger!*" she yelled again.

The car paused as if debating whether to confront her or not, but then sped up again and went off in a roar. As it passed the end of the drive, Leonora saw Bob giving her an angry and disbelieving stare, but she didn't care about that. Behind him, the car seat was laden with his belongings that used to be part of their lives together, but she didn't care about that either.

What she did care about was this: in the passenger seat, blonde brassy hair pulled up into a ponytail and wearing the kind of bright red lipstick Leonora thought had gone out in the 1980s, sat The Woman. She looked to be glowing with triumph. She'd been here, with him, all along. While Bob was collecting his things and leaving his wife, with no hope of return, *she* had been here. Egging him on. Witnessing Leonora's complete humiliation from the safety of the car.

For Leonora, this was the final straw. She ran out into the middle of the road and yelled at the departing vehicle.

"You bloody, *bloody* bastard! You don't deserve me! I'm glad you're gone and make sure you don't ever come back!"

Then, head held high, she swung round, gave a hard stare to every curtain she could see twitching, daring all the bloody neighbours to make a thing of it. If they had the courage.

They didn't. Which, under the circumstances, was probably wise.

As suddenly as it had arrived, the murderous rage left her, and she began to shake once more. Walking with as much steadiness as she could manage, Leonora picked up her plant pot, pushed the bulbs back inside what little soil was left and made her way, head still high, back down her driveway and into her home.

It was only when the door clicked shut behind her that Leonora's legs finally gave way. She wondered if she would cry, but this time she didn't. Instead, she sank slowly to the hallway floor, clutching the plant pot in her arms and trying to work out how she felt and what to do now. With her marriage, with her life, and with everything.

Chapter Eight

February into March

Selena

When Selena had returned from her first viewing of the would-be theatre, she'd cleared space in her workshop and had lain down on the floor to think. She never closed her eyes when she did this as she might miss the colours and shapes when they floated by. She had her best dreams when her eyes were open. Her workshop was a long room that she'd made by knocking down a wall between bedrooms, so was double-aspect and east/west facing, which meant the light quality was just about perfect. She'd painted the walls a soft shade of white and had installed a table for drawing designs and costume-making, as well as adding her trusty sewing machine and two mannequins for checking the flow of material.

Also in her special place were a small desk with a laptop in the corner opposite the mannequins, and her all-important coffee machine. Everything she loved and needed was here.

At the theatre, she'd picked up on strong hints of blue and cream and gold. No, not *just* gold. That was too simple. And neither Max nor Grant the set designer were simple men. The theatre wasn't a simple building and Wilde's play wasn't a simple play. Perhaps gold shot through with red would be better. Yes. That felt perfect. She knew a couple of dyers who could work something up for her. She should check with Grant and then ring them.

But not yet. It was no good attempting to rush the process. Instead, she gazed up at her ceiling and watched the colours swirling gently past. She was just getting seriously into the zone when her mobile rang.

Damn it! She should have switched it to silent or turned the darn thing off. With a sigh, Selena scrabbled in her pocket to see who it was. She didn't recognise the number, but she thought she should answer it and see if it was a real person or a scammer. She didn't want to miss out on any business.

"Hello?" she said. "Can I help you?"

A familiar voice filled her ear. "Hello, again! Is that Selena the utterly marvellous costume designer?"

Despite everything, Selena had to smile. She wasn't convinced this particular individual needed a phone at all. Surely the whole of London could hear him.

"Hello, Grant. Yes, it's me. How can I help?"

"Oh no need to worry, dear lady. I was merely ringing to see if I had the right details on my phone. Max reassured me I did but I'd always rather find out these things for myself and he said it would be fine to ring you."

"Yes, the details are perfect and here I am," Selena began to say but her words were washed away by the tide of Grant's enthusiasm.

"I must say once again how lovely it was to meet you earlier today, and so sorry I had to rush away like that. But things are always so busy-busy in the world of creativity. People have no idea! Anyway, enough about all that. The reason I'm ringing is I wanted to say again how excited I am to be working with you on Max's lovely play. I'm sure that together the two of us will make it a spectacle not to be missed! Though of course he has given us a tricky little deadline to work towards. That's Max all over, of course. Has an idea and then wants it to be done immediately. Possibly before he's even thought of it. Though, to be fair, maybe he's wiser than I think as he does always manage to make a project fly. A mover and a shaker, that's our Max. He's certainly made me have at least a thousand ideas – maybe even a million! – since I had to duck out of our meeting, my dear. Which brings me to what I was ringing you about. I've so many thoughts about what we could do in that glorious old building and how beautiful it could be. But the last thing I want to do – the last thing Max needs! – is for the set to clash with the costumes. The horror of it! Can you imagine the reviews? Frightful, my dear, frightful. So just tell me this one thing if you know it by now, though of course you might not. Do you have any ideas as to the colour scheme you're planning?"

It was astonishing how Grant appeared to have said all this in one breath alone. Selena felt both highly amused and highly exhausted at the same time. But not in a bad way. She coughed to give herself a chance to gather her thoughts and to allow the colours to settle within her mind. It would be no project at all without them.

"It's early days, Grant," she said. "And this may well change in some fashion, as I do need to give it more attention, but my first thoughts were to focus on cream and blue and gold, with red in it. I think there should definitely be a shot of red through the gold, as it's such a rich play, and a beautiful building, and it deserves it."

A brief but not unwelcome silence and then Grant gave a purr of satisfaction. "Mmm, *yes*, that sounds utterly marvellous, my dear.

And so very suitable for Wilde. If the old bugger was alive today, he would be more than happy with that. And those colours would make fantabulous scenery, as well as gorgeous costumes. Honestly, I can almost see it now. Well, thank you so much, dear Selena. You are a genius, just as Max said you were. And I will hurry along and start to make plans. Be in touch later. Thank you and bye-bye, my dear!"

And then he finished the call. Selena couldn't help laughing. There was something about Grant she liked, and even more so because of the wild fireworks of colours he carried with him. And there was also something about Max she liked as well, a little voice in her head reminded her as the colours in her mind grew stronger.

For a moment she wondered about doing more meditating to see what other ideas might come up, but Grant's phone call and his enthusiasm had given her more inspiration which needed to be grappled with. She could always meditate later. Over the years, she'd learnt that every project was different in the way it worked out and how it came to fruition, so there was no harm in mixing things up once in a while. The last thing she wanted to do was become stale.

So she opened the cupboard where she kept her store of drawing papers and took the top set of them. She spread them out across the large sunlit table where she did her work and retrieved her set of coloured pencils and crayons from the drawer.

She took these out from their packaging and laid them, organised by colour, at the end of the table, next to the first sheet of paper. Blue, cream and gold, together with red, were the ideas she'd had, the ideas she'd shared with Grant. So she put those colours first in the rows, followed by the others: green and brown; purple and pink; black and white.

Then Selena hesitated. Always at this first practical point in the whole creating process, she felt both excited and very, *very* afraid. As if she'd taken herself up to the top of a high mountain, carrying absolutely nothing with her apart from the clothes she was wearing, with the sole intention of flinging herself off that mountain top with no idea of what might lie below. No idea whether there would be safety or disaster. The damn thing never got any easier either, even though it was subtly – oh so subtly – different in every individual project she took part in.

She took a breath and then she picked up the first pencil – a blue one – and began to draw. And then, as it always did, things began to come clear and the colours began to settle into something like peace within her heart.

Selena drew a dress, perfect for summer and perfect for one of the young heroines of Wilde's play, Cecily Cardew. Something light and with chiffon and lace. Floaty and summery in blue and gold, yes, but sparky too, as the character in question was no pushover. And certainly wasn't to be underestimated. She wondered briefly if she should draw a matching floral hairband to go with the dress, but then she shook her head with a smile. No, she wasn't creating designs for a Shakespearean comedy, was she! No floral hairbands for Wilde's cast. They were too sophisticated.

It was odd she hadn't started with the men in the play, however. Usually she went from the beginning and drew her ideas for each character as they appeared. The script had been one of the first attachments Max had sent her in his emails, but in fact she already had a copy of all Oscar Wilde's plays in one volume. It had been given to her a long time ago by her mother and Selena loved it for this reason. She'd reread the play only a couple of days ago and once again it had made her smile. But it was the women within it who'd caught her attention most of all and she supposed that was why she'd started her designs with them. The older she became, the more Selena reckoned women's voices and women's wisdom should be heard more clearly across the world. And that, for her, also came down to what they wore and how they wore it. Not that the menfolk didn't have a say also – Selena was all for equality – but, for her, women mattered more, and always would.

And so for the rest of that week and most of the month, Selena had communed with the colours that filled her thoughts and surroundings, and had concentrated entirely on the upcoming play. She'd produced sketch after sketch, and worked with the fabrics she'd ordered, stitching and unpicking and rethinking. She'd taken measurements of the cast, and then sewed and altered and recut and sewed again. There had been lots of emails between Max, Grant and herself, a fair few rushed face-to-face meetings, usually at the theatre, and at least a thousand inbox downloads to mull over.

She'd loved it. She was beginning to think that this project might be the best she'd ever been involved in. The three of them seemed to spark ideas from each other as if there was no end to them, and the colours around her were surely the happiest they'd ever been: yellow and the palest blue, rose-pink and cream. Selena didn't think she'd experienced quite that gorgeous blend of colours in her mind before and she hoped it would continue. At least for as long as it took to get this project completed.

*****

March

Now, today, Selena was in the attic rooms of the theatre. Max had been busy and Selena was quickly realising he didn't mess around when it came to work. The downstairs area where the performances would take place had been cleaned and scrubbed to within an inch of its life, and a fresh coat of off-white paint added to the walls. Such simple things to do and yet they'd had a powerful effect, making the light streaming in from the windows far more vibrant. Not only that, but the kitchen and office rooms had been tidied and repainted and – most importantly of all – the attic rooms were exactly how Selena needed them to be: cleared of old machinery and still with those tables large and long enough to take the whole cast top to tail if they ever wanted to do such an extraordinary thing. This idea made her laugh, as the actors she was getting to know weren't the easiest of people and probably wouldn't take any instruction from her. She was a long way down the pecking order in the world of acting.

Grant had been busy too, marking out the stage areas with Max and bringing in backdrops and props which Max either signed off or shook his head at. Max was doing the exact same thing with Selena's costumes as well and she'd already told him several times how much better that made everything. There was nothing worse than a client who couldn't decide or who changed their minds at the last minute (though of course there was still time for that, wasn't there!) or even couldn't bring themselves to tell her they didn't like something but simply went along with it in spite of all reason. In those circumstances, Selena always realised something was wrong. The colours became flat and dull around the client, so it had been more than obvious that conversations had needed to take place.

Now, because of Max, working was far more exciting and much more enjoyable. Oh yes. Very enjoyable indeed.

Almost unbeknown to herself, Selena was humming as she worked on alterations for the male lead's shirt. Humming and smiling. It was a soft sound, certainly not loud enough to drown the rumble of voices coming from downstairs as the afternoon rehearsals continued. But just loud enough to reach the ears of the two young teenage girls Grant had found to help out in the costume department. When they heard the sound, the two girls – whose names were Poppy and Amy, and who were identical twins so it was always hard to know which was which, even for them – glanced up from their measuring task and smiled at each other before returning to their work once more. They liked working for Selena as she didn't insist on finding out all about them and helping them to be more sociable. They were perfectly happy as they were.

Selena sensed their eyes briefly on her but didn't look up. The twins were good workers. Quiet but industrious. She liked that. They also listened well to her instructions and asked a sensible question or two if they didn't fully understand something. Which was much better than ruining a task by doing it wrong. She couldn't exactly tell them apart as the colours surrounding them were so similar: soft grey and lemon, with a flash of deepest purple every now and again.

Unusual colours, especially for fifteen-year-old girls, but Selena had never been a twin, and didn't think she'd ever met any until now. So maybe twins were different. All she knew was that one of them – who might have been Poppy but could just as easily have been Amy – had more purple in their aura and one of them more grey. Other than that, they were almost completely identical. They were second – or possibly – third cousins of Grant and were in need of a work experience project as part of their school studies. So they arrived at 2pm on a Wednesday afternoon and worked with her until 5pm. Selena had saved up simple work for them to do and had also shown them how to alter a skirt, and they'd thanked her for her efforts.

She was impressed. As these thoughts flowed gently through her mind, her humming quietened, and the twins smiled to themselves, without looking up this time. But, being twins, they knew quite well they were both smiling.

Selena knew too. Not consciously, as she was no mind-reader. She knew because of the way the colours lightened and blended with each other around the two girls. And this made her smile as well.

From downstairs, the noise from the actors rose and fell, then rose again. Selena paused in her needlework and tried to gauge whether some kind of dramatic crisis was about to occur. Then the sound of laughter, and she could relax again. A couple of weeks back, there'd been a bit of a set-to when one of the male leads had accused the other one of cramping their style in some way Selena couldn't understand. She wasn't convinced that style was anything that could be cramped. It simply existed around everyone, and couldn't be driven out. Max had stepped in and nipped this potential disaster in the bud at once, as the woman playing Gwendolen Fairfax had told her afterwards. Acting troupes were nothing if not gossipy, and nothing in this particular world was ever a secret. Or if it was, it was very soon public knowledge. Now, the two men concerned were once more the best of friends.

By the time 5pm came, which tended to coincide with a short break for the cast, Selena had altered three shirts, started three more, and had put the finishing touches to the governess's dress. It had been a good afternoon's work. The twins tidied up, thanked her politely and left for home, promising to see her again the following week. She was just returning her pieces of spare cloth to one of the drawers when a voice behind her made her jump. She'd not heard anyone coming up the attic room stairs.

"Selena?"

She swung round to see Max's head appearing in the gap. His colours seemed rather muted, but maybe it was a trick of the light.

"Oh!" she said. "You surprised me. How are things going down there?"

He laughed as he climbed up the last few steps to join her. "As well as can be expected at this point. I think the cast might be finding it a bit challenging not to have a definite stage they can perform on, but I'm hoping they'll get used to it before the first night."

"You know what they say – it'll be all right on the night – and I'm sure it will be. Besides the run doesn't start until May, so there's plenty of time."

He rolled his eyes and groaned as he wandered round the workshop space. Then he slumped down on the nearest chair and rested his head on his hands on the table.

"Real time isn't the same as acting time," he said. "You always think there's time for rehearsals, but there never is, in my experience. Each time I get started on a new theatre project, I never think it will work out, even though it has in the past. Every time.

Heaven knows why, but maybe I've just been lucky, and maybe my luck's going to run out now. And then everyone involved in this play will have lost something. Because I've *not got the talent I need to keep it all together and make it work*."

He stopped speaking at once as if he'd said too much and at the same time not enough. Selena stared at him for a moment, her heart pounding, and then she put down the fabric she was holding on to and padded over to the chair to stand behind him.

The colours surrounding Max were even duller and deeper than a few moments ago and were also shot through with a darker, almost black shade she'd not seen around him before. At the same time her own special colours reached out to him and wrapped round his aura, an action that startled her. She reached out and laid a gentle hand on his shoulder.

"I'm so sorry you're feeling like this," she said. "I think you take a lot on with these projects but, from your past productions and all the wonderful reviews they've received, I think you need to give yourself a break every now and again, and trust yourself more. Besides, it's not just you doing this by yourself. There are the actors, there's Grant, there's me, and the twins of course. That's a good team to have, come what may."

Another few moments of silence and then Max sat up again, reached across and patted her hand where it still lay on his shoulder. There was a flash of colour that made Selena blink and then all was as it should be.

Half-turning, he smiled. Almost. "Thanks. You're right. Of course you are. Sorry about that just now. It's not the image I like to convey. I'm supposed to be inspiring confidence in the team so they can do their best, not acting like a wet puppy. Apologies."

Selena moved so she was standing next to him, half-leaning against the table. "Don't be sorry. Everyone's human. We all have up times and down times. They're there to be celebrated or lived through, that's all there is to it. Anyway, don't you Americans know all about coping with emotions? Far better than we Brits do!"

She'd hoped to lighten the mood by her final words, and it did make Max's smile a more honest one.

"Don't believe everything you read in the media," he replied, getting up and running one hand through his hair. "But thanks for the advice. Appreciate it. I actually didn't come up here to say that, so goodness only knows where that all came from. It's just a bad day. No, I came up to see you for another reason entirely."

"And what was that?" Selena asked.

Max paused and looked at her. "I know you work till close of play on Wednesdays so you're included in my pizza order for the team after rehearsals. But when that's done, would you like to go for a post-work drink?"

Selena gazed back at him. "Of course. I'm happy to discuss more costume options. It's not a problem. Sometimes it's good to have an informal chat to come up with more ideas."

Max coughed and looked away for a moment. "No, Selena. I don't mean as a work thing. I mean as a personal thing. I don't know how it works with you Brits over here, but in the States, we call it *going on a date*. Is that acceptable to you?"

She couldn't help but laugh, even as she felt a blush reddening her skin. "Then, yes, this Brit over here is happy to accompany you to your post-work drink event and *not* discuss work matters with you. At all. Thank you very much."

He smiled, the twinkle in his eyes all the colours of the rainbow and more. "Good, that's settled then. I'll see you later, Selena. Best get back to the madhouse down below before they start doing something really strange."

And then he turned and vanished away down the stairs and back to the stage. Selena stood looking after him, appreciating the colours that swirled and danced in his wake: red and gold, crimson, green and the kind of sunshine-yellow she'd not seen before in him. Happy colours indeed. It had been several months – nearly a year! – since she'd been out on a date and she needed to break that run. Just because she was well into her fifties didn't mean she couldn't have a good time.

Taking out her mobile, she debated whether or not to text the news of this unexpected event to her two friends but, after a moment or two, she decided against it. Leonora was too raw from the marriage disasters with pesky Bob, even in spite of her friend telling Dotts she was happy to hear about any budding romance that would take her mind off her marriage.

And Dotty herself? Well, she'd never been the kind of woman to pay much attention to romance. Though, lately with that barman giving Dotts the eye at their Friday get-togethers, you never really knew. Still, neither Leonora nor Dorothea were the right people to contact with this news, so she'd have to keep it to herself for now. Damn it. Selena knew she was many things but she wasn't a natural at *not* talking about something. Not at all.

As the rehearsals started up again downstairs, she returned to her fabric and began altering and stitching once more. This time, however, her smile was much wider as she worked, and the tune she was unconsciously humming was distinctly louder. If the twins had still been there, they would have been giggling and talking their strange secret language behind their hands.

It was odd how the early evening session seemed to last a lifetime before pizza time arrived dead on 8pm. By then Selena had visited the loos to check her appearance at least ten times, each time telling herself not to be so ridiculous and to simply enjoy the evening for whatever it turned out to be. She had nothing to prove, she knew her own worth very well. Still, she put her thick red hair into a bun twice and then shook it free twice more before she was satisfied with it. She always preferred it down. She was convinced she produced her best costumes when her hair was free.

Free the hair and free the mind, she told herself and smiled.

Pizza time was held in the kitchen – God forbid that any of Grant's precious stage area should be defiled by food stains – and was a raucous affair. Selena had conversations with all the main actors and listened with amusement to yet more drama gossip. She'd never been this much involved in a production before as, mostly, she was only called in for measuring and fitting the cast. But Max had been determined from the outset that she was part of the same team as all of them, and she liked the camaraderie this approach created. It made ideas far easier to grasp.

So she responded with various amounts of compassion and interest to the tales of acting angst. These included lines that were impossible to learn, directors from previous productions who were best avoided, the most reliable Uber drivers, what this year's pantomime season was set to be like and – worst of all! – the nearby B&B where cockroaches were provided alongside the soap and towels.

And, all the time, Selena kept giving secret glances towards Max as he joined in with the gossip and offered solutions to those in need of advice. More often than not, she found he was also taking sneaky glances at her, which was both flattering and disconcerting at the same time. She felt like a teenager again. Perish the thought!

It was past 9pm by the time everyone had tidied up and disappeared off home, or more probably to their favourite wine bars. The acting tribe wasn't known for getting early nights, and this lot certainly knew how to party. Selena wondered what the end of show celebration would be like, if indeed they had anything to celebrate. She was sure it would be fine – there was something about the way the colours and the sparks blended together that made her feel that everything would work out well. And her gut instincts had never been wrong yet.

Selena grabbed her jacket where she'd left it on a nearby chair. Then she smiled at Max as he turned round from giving the sink a quick wipe down.

"Time for our non-work related drink then?" she asked.

He nodded. "Definitely. I'm sure we both deserve it."

As she shrugged her jacket on, Max reached out to help her with the sleeve and there it was again: that bright flash of gold and purple when he touched her. It startled her.

"Everything okay?" he asked.

"Oh yes," she replied, shaking the colours away. "Just wondering where the cast have gone. The night is young, and we might well end up at the same pub."

He gave her a quizzical look. "Would that bother you?"

"No," she said. "Not at all. But don't you have to maintain a veneer of unapproachability in order to inspire your actors to obey all your directing decisions? If they think you're chatting up the dressmaking totty, then you might lose some respect."

She gazed at him, trying to maintain a straight face for as long as she could. But she lost it, and began to laugh helplessly at his utterly puzzled expression.

A moment ticked by and then he began to laugh too.

"Got you!" she said between gusts of laughter. "I really had you going then. You actually thought I meant it. Oh, that was wonderful. *Wonderful.*"

She wiped her tears away, and saw Max was rolling his eyes to the ceiling.

"Yes," he admitted. "You had me believing you there. In every way. Is this what you Brits call *sarcasm* then? I'd better know from the outset so I can be prepared next time."

Still half-laughing and secretly pleased at the concepts of *outset* and *next time*, even before they'd started on this date, Selena nodded. "Yes. It's sarcasm. Welcome to Britain."

Outside the theatre, Selena waited for Max to lock up and set the alarm, and then they wandered down the street together, walking side by side. Not touching exactly, but close. The night wasn't cold, but Selena was still glad of her jacket.

"Where are we going?" she asked after a few minutes as they approached the junction at the end of the street. There was a steady amount of traffic, but then again this was London. There was always traffic at any time of the night or day. It never stopped. Well apart from during Covid lockdowns, Selena reminded herself. It had stopped then and the whole of London had lost something of its spirit and zest for life. It had been unsettling and she'd realised for the first time how much inspiration the city gave her for her designs. Nothing she created could be created in a void. Her ideas, her thoughts, her inspiration came not just from within herself but from her interaction with the city she loved and lived in. Because London carried its own energy, through its buildings, its people, its cars, its ever-present buzz. This was the energy that sparked with her own so she could recreate her own self and create her own special craft. Her life was in this city and, when it had fallen silent during that peculiar time, so her inspiration and designs had fallen silent too. When it came back to life, the colours and shapes and ideas returned to her and she could start again.

She'd welcomed them like old friends. Just as Max opened his mouth to reply to her question, the realisation hit her like a sudden rain shower. She had the exact same feeling from walking with Max along the road now as she'd had when her inspiration had begun again: the feeling of an old friend returning just when she most needed it.

"I know a place a couple of blocks from here," he said. "A small bar but it serves good coffee too. Decaff even. How does that suit? It's not the usual theatre tribe place either, so my reputation might remain intact for another night."

Selena smiled. "Ah. Sarcasm, I see. I'm prepared to be impressed. And it sounds like it will suit very well, thank you."

"That's a relief," he said. "I hope you like it."

They continued walking, taking a couple of turns that led them into an alleyway Selena had never noticed before. It was framed by a line of terraces on the left, and a wall on the right.

"There's a private park behind the wall," Max commented. "It belongs to the bar and they open it twice a year. On midsummer day and at Christmas, or so they tell me. It's supposed to be very beautiful, but I've never seen it for myself."

He stopped outside a green door and rapped the panels twice before turning the handle.

"Do they need to know we're coming?" Selena asked, amused, as he stepped to one side and waved her in.

"No, not really," he laughed. "It's just that sometimes the tables are set up quite close to the door, and I don't want to startle anyone."

He was right too. Selena only just managed to squeeze in. She found herself between one group of youngish men dressed entirely in black and another group of older women (though not as old as she was) who were all wearing very sparkly and very pink jumpers.

"Hello!" these women chorused as they raised their champagne glasses in Selena's direction. "Welcome to Iris's Bar. Are you new? How lovely!"

"She's with me," Max replied as he clicked the door shut behind them. "This is Selena and she's designing costumes for my new play. Selena, these ladies are part of the Wednesday Night Cinema Club. They always come here for a quick drink after the film."

"And tonight you have to guess which film we've just been to see!" the tallest of the sparkly ladies said. "Though we hope that's not too difficult."

Selena couldn't help laughing. "Well, I think – and I know I'm only taking a guess as I've not seen it myself – I *think* you might have been watching *Barbie*?"

"You got it!"

"Yes, success!"

"We are fully immersed in Barbie World!"

"Good," said Selena. "As long as it's full of colour, then that's the world for me."

The bar was certainly full of colour too. Selena could see bright patterns of cream and orange, blue and purple, green and (yes!) pink, all of them dancing happily and gently together. It gave her a strong sense of hope. As if anything might happen and it would always be positive.

"And these good men," said Max as he took her arm and turned her round to the other table near the door. "These men are the Goth Society. They're usually here on a Wednesday too."

The four men Max had indicated solemnly raised their pint glasses to greet her, and Selena, just as solemnly, nodded back. With a smile aimed at both her and them, Max guided her through the room to the bar. There Selena caught a glimpse of a very wrinkled female face with the bluest pair of eyes she'd ever seen. Not only that, but the colours dancing round this woman were all the shades of blue that Selena had ever imagined. She'd never met anyone whose aura was one colour and one colour alone. People's auras were usually a mixture, because people themselves were a mixture, of good and bad, dark and light. It had always been that way.

But not so here and not so tonight.

"Hello," Selena said as she gazed at the face. "I'm Selena and I'm here with Max. Thank you so much for allowing me into your bar. You must be Iris. It's a pleasure to meet you."

The blue eyes gazing back at her crinkled up into a smile. "Likewise, Selena. I am indeed Iris, and it's a pleasure to meet you too. Thank you for visiting us. Now, what is it I can get you? Mr

Max, I trust you are paying for this lady. Seeing as you've brought her here on a first date."

"How do you know that?" Selena asked. "Even I didn't know about it until earlier today."

The face gave her a solemn wink. "It's the magic of my bar, my dear."

"Not to mention the fact that I've been talking to Iris about asking you out for at least a week now," Max cut in. "She knows all my secrets."

"And they're all absolutely safe with me when they need to be," Iris replied. "Now, drinks orders, please!"

Max gave their order of a small white wine and a large red one, and then pointed to a table for two at the furthest side of the bar. "How about there? If you grab it, I'll bring the drinks over."

"Looks perfect," Selena said, with a smile. "Plus it's the only table that's free so definitely the best choice."

"I made sure it was left free for you," Iris's voice echoed from behind the bar as she fulfilled the order. "I know what's good for my customers."

"Thank you," Selena said and trotted off to the table.

As she sat down and put her jacket on the back of the chair, she puzzled over the bar-owner's words. The table bore no Reserved sign, so Iris must have been joking. Unless she'd been moving people along to other tables until she and Max had arrived. But that didn't seem to be the landlady's style.

As she waited for Max to join her, Selena looked around the bar. Not counting the cinema ladies and the Goth lads, there were about four other tables in the room. Two of them had couples sitting at them who – at her best guess – were on a date in the same way as she was, but probably not their first date. At the third table sat a serious-looking white-haired man who was making notes from a newspaper into a journal and, at the fourth, sat three men who appeared to be on a low-key boys' night out, judging by the line of glasses next to them. They weren't being particularly rowdy, which was a good thing. Selena doubted whether Iris would allow any rowdiness in her bar. She didn't have that vibe.

In fact, the whole aura of the bar – if bars were allowed to have auras – was one of comfort and happiness. The walls were painted a very pale yellow and were full of pictures of the countryside, which made Selena smile as here they were in the middle of London. The tables had yellow and gold tablecloths with blue upholstered chairs. Selena knew quite well how 1990s this scheme was but she liked it nonetheless. If something worked, then to her mind it was timeless.

"Here you are," Max said as he returned to the table with what looked to be the largest buckets of wine Selena had ever seen. "Wine as requested."

Selena started to laugh. "You're telling me that's a small white wine?"

Max grinned back at her as he sat down, the colours around him swirling a little before settling themselves. "I don't think Iris knows how to pour a small glass of anything, but you don't have to drink it all if you don't want to."

"Oh I think I can manage perfectly well," Selena replied with a wave to the bar owner, who was now leaning against the bar and surveying her domain. "Besides, I don't think I'd dare leave anything Iris has offered me."

At that, the woman in question turned and looked across at the two of them. "I should hope not!" she said.

Left alone, Selena and Max sipped their drinks. The wine was rich, the flavours bursting on her tongue and setting up their own waterfall of colour.

"This is good," she said. "Why on earth haven't I found this place before?"

"Iris always says people find her bar when they need it most. Certainly I stumbled across it when I was probably at my lowest ebb and I felt I'd found a home, of sorts. It helped me get my head together again."

Selena reached out and patted his arm. Once more that sudden flash of merging colours but it was gentler now.

"What happened?" she asked him.

He grimaced and put down his glass. "It was four years ago. My father died unexpectedly – of cancer – when we thought he was in remission. He and I had plans to go travelling in the fall and I never thought … I never thought he wouldn't be there. Anyway, it was grim. For the whole family and especially for my mother. After the funeral, I stayed with her for a while – my brother and sister live in Europe, so I'm the one who's closest to home. Then she basically got sick of me and told me to go back to work. That's my mom all over, really. And I had a London trip coming up for a theatre conference, so I came. Over here, I don't know, there was just something which seemed to put me right back to that moment when I found out about my father. And I was wandering around, just keeping moving so I didn't catch up with myself, and I found Iris and her bar. God knows why I walked in this direction, but I did, and I'm very glad about it. Ever since then, I've been coming back here whenever I'm in the city, and the welcome is always the same."

"I'm so very sorry," Selena said quietly when Max had finished speaking. "That's a terrible thing to happen."

He nodded. "Thank you. But I'm sorry for offloading all that on you – I hadn't meant to say quite so much. It must be Iris's influence."

"Nonsense!" Selena replied. "Talking about the things that matter is always worthwhile, so there's no need to apologise for anything. If there was more openness and honesty in the world, then there would be far less pain and conflict. In my view. And I happen to think it's a jolly wise view too."

Max blinked at her and then laughed. "That's what I really like about you, Selena!"

"Oh? What's that then?"

"Your ability to leap from saying something serious to saying something witty in less than a second. It's a real skill."

"Something I learnt from my mother," Selena replied. "A very long time ago."

"Ah," he said. "Is your mother no longer with us then?"

She shook her head and took another sip of that glorious wine before replying. "Sadly not. She died when I was sixteen. In a car crash. Not her fault. She was walking to the shops and a car mounted the pavement and killed her outright. It was deeply and truly shocking, and it took me a long time to get over it. So I understand what you mean about your father."

Max didn't reply at first to the revelation Selena hadn't known she would say. Instead, he reached for her hand and took it between both of his. At once the colours which had been flowing around the both of them deepened and flared, and she felt something warm her to the bones. It made her smile, even amongst the sadness she still felt about that terrible day.

Then he let her go.

"I'm sorry too," he said.

The warmth from his touch was enveloping her both inside and out and it took her a moment to recover.

"Thank you," she said.

After that, the conversation moved on to subjects less close to their hearts. Selena laughed at Max's stories about growing up in the States and trying to find his niche in life. His first job had been in motor insurance which had been a surprise as he wasn't a huge fan of cars. From there, he'd moved over to accident insurance but this was pretty grim most of the time. Whilst working, he was already getting involved in local theatres – sometimes acting, but mainly working backstage. It had slowly but surely become his life, taking his mind away from the daily grind of his job. Then he'd had the opportunity to take a theatre studies course at night school and hadn't looked back.

"Mind you," he said with a wry smile. "My first job was looking after the animals who were the real stars of one of our local Christmas revues, so I spent a lot of time shit-shovelling. It's astonishing how much one small donkey can produce."

"I can imagine!"

In turn, Selena told him about how she'd always loved fabric as a young girl, as far back as she could remember, and it had been the one career path she'd always wanted to follow. One of her earliest and very special memories was of being allowed to play with her grandmother's old scarves and shoes, of which there were many.

"She had all the colours I could have dreamed of," Selena recalled, unable to keep the smile from her face. "Gorgeous golds and creams, and vibrant greens and reds. She loved her colours. And the material she had too – all those silken scarves and beautiful leather shoes. Honestly, I've not thought about them for years. I loved playing with them, draping myself in those scarves – all the colours all at once too! – and then prancing around in shoes far too big for me. It was astonishing I didn't do myself an injury, but somehow I never did."

"We were all tougher as children, I'm sure of it," Max agreed. "From what you say, you must take after your grandmother. I mean it's obvious how much you love your colours and fabrics. I envy you a little too – knowing from being a child what you want to do in life is pretty damn wonderful. You're very lucky."

"Thank you," Selena replied. "But we all have different paths. Who's to say that your life would have been better if you'd gone straight into theatre work from the beginning? Sometimes it's the journey that counts just as much as the destination."

Max raised his glass to her. "Good point! You sound exactly like Iris, which is always a good thing."

"But of course," said the lady herself who suddenly appeared at their table to collect the now empty glasses. "Nothing could be better than sounding like me."

And Selena and Max couldn't help but agree. As it was now getting on for 11pm (how had the time flown so much, Selena wondered), they both decided not to opt for another drink but to make their way home. Max offered to give her a lift in the car he somehow found a place to park each day near the theatre, but she decided on an Uber. She didn't want to feel obliged to invite him in.

Not that Selena *didn't* want to invite him home (quite the contrary, really!), but she wanted to give herself time to think about this date and what it might mean. Max waited with her for her taxi, and the silence between them was an easy one. When the Uber arrived, she turned to him, kissed him on the cheek and smiled at his pleased expression.

"That was a lovely day," she said. "Thank you. I'm happy to have found Iris's bar and I'm even happier to have spent time with you. I would love to do the same. Would a Saturday sometime suit you? I'd like to show you some of the parts of London I know and love too."

"Yes, I'd love that," he said with a smile. "It sounds perfect. Let's arrange something very soon, Selena."

With that, he leant forward and kissed her on the cheek in return and then watched as she got into the taxi. She felt his eyes like a caress on her skin and thought that their next meeting couldn't come quickly enough.

When the cab set off, she turned and waved until the end of the street, and was glad to see him waving back. It gave her a feeling of hope she hadn't had for a while, and which she hadn't realised had been missing in the first place.

From the start of the year, when everything had been difficult and painful for those she loved, Selena saw how the colours were changing and she needed to be open to them once more. She was ready.

Chapter Nine

March

Dorothea

Monday morning and Dorothea was not at her best. Her alarm hadn't gone off and she'd woken up ten minutes later than usual. As a result, she'd not had time to give Oscar his five-minute cuddle which had made her temperamental cat distinctly out of sorts. On the plus side, she'd still had time to feed him so his complaints about her service should be minimal. She'd also failed to iron her blouse properly and had been forced to run for her car whilst eating a banana for breakfast. She then raced to the train station at rather more than the legal speed limit, and had to run to get the train too.

To cap it all, she'd forgotten to bring her book and so was forced to stare out of the window for the entire commute rather than immersing herself in the world of her current read.

All very unsatisfactory. And, last night, she'd been awake for a long while worrying about Bob and his new life, and how it affected her friends. A large part of this was the one important fact she'd been keeping from both Leonora and Selena, and which was weighing heavily on her shoulders. So much so that late last night when she should really have been getting ready for bed, she'd rung her brother and had had a long and very unsatisfactory conversation with him. It was this which had kept her awake and it was this which had given her such a poor start to the morning.

If only Bob would do the right thing or, at the very least, listen to his sister, she wouldn't be feeling so out-of-sorts now. Family! They were simply terrible. How she longed to shake some sense into her brother.

Dorothea wished she had someone to confide in, but she didn't. The only two people in the world she could talk to were Selena and Leonora. And she absolutely couldn't talk to them about this. It would be unfair on every level. It was up to Bob to resolve the situation. She hoped he would do so soon.

All these thoughts continued to plague Dorothea as the train made its steady and familiar way out of the English countryside and towards the heart of the city. Funny how commuting was never a problem for her. Several people at work – some colleagues and some passing acquaintances – had commented recently how commuting was for young people and she must be tired of the daily journey into the office. But Dorothea didn't see it like that. She loved her routine and getting up early was never – well, apart from today! – an issue for her. The journey didn't make her feel tired. She enjoyed reading, and the opportunity to lose herself in a book at the start and end of the working day was always a pleasure. Not today of course, sadly.

Yes, the tube journey wasn't pleasant at the best of times. But she didn't have to travel too many stops, and the walk from the tube station to her office was a chance to get some air before work began. She wasn't complaining.

Dorothea also knew how lucky she was to enjoy her job so much. She'd been a civil servant in the Business and Trade Department for years now – more years than she cared to remember – and she found her life's meaning in the simple routine of it all. She wasn't a high-flier and she certainly didn't have the secret career Selena always insisted she must have, but it was enough for her. Most of her days were spent dealing with the vast selection of queries about business and national trade law which arrived in the team's inbox. Most she could answer, but some were passed onto one of the team specialists for them to respond more fully. In those circumstances, Dorothea always followed up with the expert to ensure the response had been sent out on time, and also to educate herself. She liked learning things. She also helped organise conferences both internally and externally. These were a challenge but she thrived on it. Not the working life her good friends seemed to suspect she had, but it suited her well.

This morning, Dorothea arrived at her office five minutes before her official start time. It was a relief not to be late and she was more than glad she'd made her train. She'd be sure to give Oscar extra cuddle time tonight to make up for abandoning him this morning. If of course he was minded to forgive her, though a handful or two of treats would help to bring him round.

At the department's entrance, Dorothea keyed in the code and pushed open the door. Inside, there was a subtle scent of lavender from the polish used by the early morning cleaners who had already completed their work. Sometimes, Dorothea wondered about paying for a cleaner at home herself, but it would only make her feel guilty. It wasn't as if she didn't have time for domestic chores.

As Dorothea walked across the entrance hall and towards the lift, the receptionist – Katy – glanced up and gave her a warm smile.

"Morning, Dorothea!"

"Morning, Katy," Dorothea replied. "Good weekend?"

"Yes, thank you. And you?"

Dorothea nodded. "Fine, thank you."

And that was the customary greeting done. A simple but pleasing exchange for both women. Dorothea was about to continue on her way when Katy – much to her surprise – spoke again.

"Oh, I forgot to say," the receptionist added. "There's a meeting for all staff today at 10am. In the main boardroom. I've been told to tell everyone as they arrive, though there's an email in everyone's inboxes as well."

"Thank you," said Dorothea. "Any idea what it's about?"

Katy shook her head. "The email doesn't say. But I'm sure it will all be explained later."

"Yes, I'm sure it will," Dorothea agreed with a smile.

And that was that. Dorothea wasn't unduly concerned. The civil service liked to get people together for announcements every now and again which, in her view, could just as easily be done over email. They probably thought it helped with the team spirit and perhaps they were right; such meetings always came with coffee, tea and snacks so it was a chance to catch up with colleagues you might not have seen for a while. It was the way the management liked to do things.

In her shared office, Dorothea smiled at the couple of people who were already in and typing furiously at their desks, and agreed with them both that, yes, the weekend had been good but not long enough. It was the kind of conversation she had every Monday morning with the team, but in fact Dorothea was quite happy with the length of the weekend. Two days sorting out the house and the garden and getting to grips with her current book were more than enough, and she liked coming in to start the new week on a Monday.

This wasn't the type of conversation that went down well, however, so she'd learnt to keep that particular opinion to herself.

Dorothea took off her jacket, hung it up on the office coat rack and sat down. She switched on her computer and checked her emails to see what had come in over the weekend. Apart from the meeting invitation for this morning – which she'd reply to in a minute – it looked like there was nothing terribly urgent so she could just get on with her day. This was a blessing. Dorothea didn't like emergency emails that had to be dealt with immediately as she thought it was better by far to give a problem some thought before coming up with a solution.

She was about to click on the meeting request when the office assistant brought her a steaming mug of coffee.

"Thanks, Maddy," she said. "You're a mind-reader."

Maddy – the latest in a long line of office assistants who only held the post for six months or so until getting reallocated to the team that needed them the most – smiled back. "No problem! Let me know if you need anything for this meeting we're all having later."

"I don't think there's anything to do for that one," Dorothea replied. "From what Katy was saying, I believe it's one where we just turn up and listen, but I'll check."

Quickly, she opened the invitation and looked through. It was as the receptionist had said, with no further details attached. This in itself was unusual, as management preferred to at least give the staff a clue as to what any meeting might be about. Dorothea assumed it was an oversight.

"No," she said to Maddy who was still hovering at the side of her desk. "Nothing to do according to the email so we'll have to wait till later."

"Oh," said Maddy. "It's just …"

"… just … what?" Dorothea prompted the younger woman gently.

"Well," Maddy leant over and lowered her voice so the rest of the team couldn't hear. "It's just that there are some rumours going around the assistants' teams and I thought you might know more about it."

"What sort of rumours?" Dorothea said with a slight frown. She didn't like the sound of that – rumours were rarely helpful in any situation and tended to make things a thousand times worse.

"Something about how the department is doing," Maddy whispered. "It was all over our WhatsApp group this morning."

Dorothea smiled. She was sure WhatsApp would have got things wrong and she herself avoided the app like the plague. She didn't think Maddy needed to worry.

"I'm sure the department is doing fine," she whispered back, keen to reassure the assistant as much as possible. "I don't think there's any need to be concerned. But let's not panic. Let's wait and see when 10am comes round. All will be revealed then."

Maddy nodded, though she didn't look convinced by Dorothea's words, and went back to her tasks. Dorothea sipped at her coffee as she got on with her day, sending smiles and nods to the remainder of the team as they arrived in the office.

By 9.30am, they were all assembled. The team Dorothea was responsible for were what she liked to call 'old-timers' as most of them had been in the role for over ten years, and they each had a huge wealth of experience to call on. The youngest of them (apart from Maddy) was Richard who was in his mid-thirties so a whole generation younger than Dorothea. He was the only one of them who had started in their team and not moved around. This was unusual as the civil service preferred staff to have a range of different skills, which could only be achieved in a variety of departments. However, Richard had come in with a business degree and lots of practical experience from working in his father's company during the holidays, so she supposed the management didn't want to lose that kind of talent.

Dorothea herself had worked in five different departments before finding her niche in the national business development office. It was her favourite job of all, and definitely better than her least favourite, which had been the tax office. She'd found that one a real struggle, though her people skills had improved hugely during her eighteen months there. Still, it wasn't a role she wished to repeat. She wasn't cut out for tax.

At 9.50am, Dorothea stopped what she was doing and locked her computer. The other members of the team were doing the same and so she waited for them to be ready before heading up to the boardroom.

Once there, Dorothea headed to the back of the room where there were enough spare seats for her team to sit together. She smiled at them in what she hoped was a reassuring way, and waited for the meeting to begin. Three members of the management team were already at the front, their shadows obscuring the presentation behind them which was currently showing the first of the slides would be presented in a few moments. The HR director was as always in these meetings sitting at one end of the long table and frowning at his mobile. Dorothea had never got on with him and sometimes wondered why a man who didn't particularly like people had ended up in HR.

She hoped that, whatever this was about, the meeting would be over soon and they could all get on with their day. She had a lot of work to sort out.

Finally, the overall director tapped on the side of his glass with his pen, brought the room to order and started the presentation.

It took an hour. This consisted of the half-hour presentation and then a barrage of questions from the floor. Dorothea listened and scribbled notes on the pad she'd brought along – even though the director had reassured them that a copy of the slides would be sent to them all as soon as the meeting was over, alongside another email from HR. As she tried to take everything in, Dorothea felt her shoulders tighten and the thud of fear in her heart. This news wasn't what she'd expected to hear. There'd been no warning. Or perhaps she'd not been paying enough attention recently. She'd certainly had other things on her mind, Bob and Leonora being the most important of these. It looked like Maddy had been right to worry.

After all the talking and discussion (some of this had been quite lively which always made Dorothea feel uncomfortable), drinks and nibbles had been laid out but nobody was in the mood to stay and chat. One or two of the younger staff did grab some biscuits or a slice of cake here and there, but they didn't stay either. Dorothea and her team made their way back to the office. They didn't talk until they were at the desks. Then there was a flurry of questions which Dorothea couldn't answer without considerably more information than had been given to them at the meeting.

Seeing quite clearly that no work was likely to be carried out for a while, she sent Maddy out to the café on the corner to get them a decent set of coffees and a box of doughnuts. Then Dorothea arranged a team meeting in their own tiny meeting room at 11.30am and printed out the slides and the promised email that HR had sent to them while they'd been away from their desks.

It made for grim reading.

Because while Dorothea had been listening to what the director was saying, she'd been selfishly hoping against hope that the plan wouldn't apply to her team and this department. Surely their expertise in business and trade matters would always be important. Surely this new programme of job re-evaluations (whatever *they* might be …) and redundancies would be focused on other departments and not on this one. But the details that hadn't been forthcoming this morning at the main meeting were right there in black and white in the email: a list of teams in line for re-evaluation and redundancy, one of which was her own.

Dorothea felt sick. She wished once more that there'd been some warning of this for team leaders such as herself, but she understood why management would judge it better to tell everyone in the building at the same time. It was an impossible choice.

Maddy returned with the coffees and the doughnuts before Dorothea had even started to think about what she should say, but that didn't matter. The 11.30am meeting was more or less as Dorothea had feared. Her team were worried, unhappy and, in the case of Richard, infuriated. She felt exactly the same way herself. But she did all she could do as a team leader: she offered what little reassurance she had; she promised support where possible; and finally and most importantly she made a note of all their questions so she could raise them and get an answer.

By lunchtime, Dorothea was shattered. The excitement of it being Monday and the start of the working week had entirely vanished.

There were at least a thousand questions buzzing in her head and she couldn't get a grip on any of them. She'd scheduled a meeting with her boss this afternoon, and had typed up the issues raised by her team and added several of her own. She'd then printed this out and placed it carefully into her handbag. She much preferred having something physical to refer to. It was so much more practical than simply adding notes to her mobile, which didn't feel as real.

At lunchtimes, Dorothea usually took a walk to the nearby park if the weather was good, buying a sandwich and some fruit from the corner shop on the way. If the weather was bad, she chose a later lunch so she would be sure to get a decent seat in the staffroom. But today she needed some air. A lot of air. And she needed to get out of the office, no matter what the weather was doing.

So she told her team she'd see them later and made her way outdoors. In the reception area, she and Katy nodded solemnly at each other, but neither woman had the heart to talk.

In the street, the air smelt of rain. She walked to the end of the road, ignoring the one or two people who passed her as she didn't recognise them. There were other offices in the area too. Not everyone here worked in the civil service.

And perhaps one day neither would she.

This thought made Dorothea feel ill again, so she put it to one side. She bought a sandwich at the shop and treated herself to a pineapple juice. Then she walked along the cut-through at the end of the road next to the sandwich shop and into the park. It wasn't a large area, but was well-kept by the council and incredibly popular with nearby workers over the summer. Any passing tourist was a rare sighting indeed.

Dorothea made her way over to the small bench at the far side of the pond. It was set back a little from the path and hidden from immediate view by two holly bushes. This meant that any casual stroller couldn't see the bench was there at all, which suited her very well – as it meant she didn't have to share the space. There was only room for two, but Dorothea always made sure to place her lunch next to her so people wouldn't be tempted to try to join her. She did so now.

As Dorothea ate her ham salad sandwich on brown, she gazed at the pond where two or three mallards were diving for their own lunch, and tried to clear her mind.

It wasn't easy. Her thoughts felt muddy and knotted. This morning's big announcement about the restructure programme had been such a shock. The email they'd all received afterwards had given them an idea of the timescale: there would be a consultation period of about a month; then two weeks of enhanced redundancy for those who wished to apply for that; then a week of decision-making; followed by a month of redundancy notices if not enough staff had been selected to take the enhanced package.

So, by the summer, everyone would know what was likely to happen to them. It felt horrible. Dorothea had always assumed she and her team, and indeed the whole building, would be safe. It was the civil service; everything remained the same and nothing ever changed. It was part of the reason she loved it so much.

A sudden flood of fear swept through her and she felt her eyes well up with tears she was determined not to shed. Because what good would crying do? It was pointless. She needed to come up with a plan for getting through the next few months and a plan to make sure she and her team survived the restructure as best they could. Dorothea still couldn't believe their department was on that list at all. They did good work and always had done.

Though they didn't create much profit. And profit had been one of the key elements in the presentation this morning, and also one of the key factors in the follow-up email. But profit wasn't the main focus of the business development team. They were there to help people and to offer legal and financial advice. They weren't focused on making money and never had been.

But times were changing. If she thought about it, Dorothea had to admit that in recent months – and perhaps even further back than that – her meetings with her boss and her regular reviews had included a conversation or three about how to make money. She'd never paid this much heed. Hadn't thought it important. She'd even assumed it was just another one of her boss's five-minute fads and had discounted it as such.

Well, perhaps she should have listened with more attention and done a whole lot more about it. Perhaps some of this was her fault after all.

Sandwich and drink forgotten, Dorothea finally gave way to tears, brushing them away furiously when she heard footsteps approaching the bench.

She was lucky. It wasn't anyone she knew from the office and they didn't even glance in her direction, which was a blessing. Dorothea was supremely uncomfortable with any personal displays of emotion, and being caught crying on a bench made her hot with embarrassment. So, once the danger was passed, she wiped her eyes, checked her appearance in her handbag mirror, gathered up her belongings, disposing of the half-eaten sandwich in a nearby bin, and returned to the office.

All that afternoon, the atmosphere in the department and throughout the whole building was a tense one. Dorothea's meeting with her immediate boss answered some of her questions but raised many more, which she tried to convey to her team once she'd returned to her desk. By now, her colleagues had moved from shock to a growing sense of anger, and Dorothea couldn't blame them. She was going through the same feelings herself. All she could do was keep reassuring them that they knew everything she did, and she was holding nothing back from them. All this at the same time as trying to keep on top of her actual work projects. Though even she had to admit that some of the enthusiasm she felt about her allocated tasks had disappeared.

She made sure she was the last person to leave the office that night and did her best to reassure the individual members of her team as they left to go home. She wasn't entirely sure how effective that was, but she knew it was her duty as their team leader.

Then, at last, she was alone. She spent some time thinking about the day and trying not to panic. Then she made sure the windows were shut and the office secure, put on her jacket, picked up her handbag and left. It was 6pm. Later than usual for her home-time but not as late as it actually felt. For Dorothea, it felt as if it was 2am and she'd been on an all-nighter for an urgent project. It was a very long time since she'd had to do that.

The reception area was only half-lit, and the security guard gave her a quick nod of recognition which she returned with a brief smile as she walked across the floor. Once outside the office, Dorothea felt the tension leave her shoulders and she stretched a little to ease her muscles.

She turned to make her way to the tube for the journey home and then hesitated. She didn't feel like going home. Not right now. She didn't want the day's difficulties to follow her and overshadow her evening. She needed to step out of her own beloved routine for a while. To get off the world temporarily before gathering her courage to get back on it again. To do something else before catching that train.

Dorothea closed her eyes for a moment. Then when she opened them, she decided what to do. It was radical – for her anyway – but it might be exactly what she needed.

So, half an hour later, she was sitting at the bar of the *Crusting Pipe* with a glass of the house white at her elbow. She'd expected to order it, find a table and sit down to enjoy her day's respite. However, much to her surprise, that hadn't happened. Because Dorothea had walked into the pub and the Australian barman had been polishing a wine glass behind the bar. He'd smiled at her and, utterly unexpectedly, she'd smiled back.

Now, she was perched on a bar stool, somewhat precariously, and sipping her drink whilst watching the world come and go. Every now and then, the barman – whose name turned out to be Tom – would have enough time for a few minutes' conversation with her which Dorothea had decided was quite nice. It gave her something else to think about apart from work.

When she'd first arrived, Tom had widened his eyes at her.

"Evening!" he'd said, putting down the glass he'd been holding. "It's not the last Friday of the month already, is it?"

"Sadly not," Dorothea replied. "Why do you say that?"

"You and your friends always come here then. You three ladies are in our band of regulars. The Friday friendship club. That's what we've called you."

Dorothea couldn't help but laugh. Which was a surprise, as she couldn't remember laughing the entire day. Then again, there'd been absolutely nothing to laugh at.

"It makes us sound very official," she said. "And we're honestly not. We've just known each other for years and it's a good chance to catch up."

"So," the barman replied. "Are you having a change of day and is it for something special? If so, I can recommend the house champagne."

She shook her head. This evening was not for champagne. Not by any stretch of anyone's imagination. "No. I'm on my own tonight. After today, I needed a drink before I catch the train home."

Tom nodded sympathetically. "Bad day? That's what we're here for. What can I get you?"

"Just the house white," she said. "As usual. But a large one, I think."

"Oh, that's different. What happened?"

Dorothea found herself laughing at his raised eyebrow. "Am I always so predictable?"

He gave her a quick grin as he retrieved the house white from the fridge. "Nothing to be worried about! People tend to stick to what they're familiar with, that's all. You always have a small glass first if you get here before your friends, and then the friendship club buy a bottle of something afterwards. It's your system."

Dorothea sighed. "I suppose it's good to have a system. But, then again, I've been an administrator all my working life, so I would say that. But I don't know if I'm going to be an administrator for much longer …"

She hadn't meant to say her last few words. She'd meant to keep her thoughts to herself. But there was something about Tom and the way he was listening to her whilst pouring the wine she ordered that made a space inside her open up. It was surprising but not uncomfortable.

"Why do you say that?" he asked as he handed her the glass.

Dorothea closed her eyes for a moment. "Because our team all found out at work today that we're in danger of being made redundant. We're going through what they're calling a *period of business restructuring* and we're one of the teams in the line of fire."

"I'm so sorry," he said. "What a shock for you."

And then, over the next hour, whilst she finished her wine and had another small glass too, Dorothea told Tom exactly what had happened. And what she felt about it as well. Somehow, he made it easy to talk. And, even better than that, talking about it made her worry slightly more bearable. Or perhaps that was the wine. Sometimes, whatever the doctors said, a glass or two of wine *was* the best medicine.

Still, at about 7.30pm, she knew it was time to go. The pub was getting more crowded, though not as crowded as it always was on a Friday. She finished her drink and waved to Tom at the other side of the bar where he'd just finished serving a group of smartly-dressed women who looked as if they were celebrating something. Lucky them.

201

He held up one finger and mouthed something at her that seemed to be urgent. So she waited as he sorted the till out before heading in her direction.

"Are you just off now?" he said.

"Yes. Thanks for listening to my long list of troubles. You didn't have to, and I do appreciate it. Very much."

"It was no problem," Tom replied with a warm smile. "Always happy to help. There was one thing though. Well, maybe two things …"

He trailed off and gave her a searching glance as if he was trying to decide whether or not to complete his sentence.

"Go on," she said. "I've given you my work life story in miniature tonight, so you're more than welcome to say whatever you like in return."

"Sure," he said. "Thanks. It's this: first of all, it's been good talking with you, but you should tell your friends what's been happening. I'm just a stranger in a bar you go to, though if I'm honest I'd like to be more than that if it's ever possible. I'd like to know you better. But that's not the main thing I wanted to say right now. You need to let your friends know what's happening because they're your friends and they know you best. The second thing is I know what's happening at your office is pretty grim but when you've got over the shock of it, you might find it's a chance to do something different with your life. It's what I did and, right now, I wouldn't want it to be any other way. Walking away from my job at home last year and deciding to travel round Europe instead was the best decision I ever made. Up to now. Anyway, I spot another keen customer, so I'd best go and serve them. It was nice talking to you, Dorothea, really nice, and I hope the rest of your week gets better. Hope to see you and your friends at your next Friday session soon."

And with that, he was gone. Dorothea was startled at what he'd said and what she thought he'd said, and wasn't even sure if she'd heard him correctly. Particularly the part about wanting to know her better. But, whatever Tom had meant by that, he was right about the need to tell her friends. And he was probably right about the possibility of seeing all this restructure as an opportunity, though she wasn't ready to do that today. And probably not for the rest of this week either, but it was certainly the best approach to take. She wondered what job he'd had in Australia and why he'd chosen – if it had been a choice – to give it up and travel instead.

There was a lot for Dorothea to ponder on, and this she did all the way home and for many days afterwards. It didn't bring her any answers but it did help. She found she was looking forward to her monthly Friday night get-together with her friends even more than she usually would.

Most of all, however, she wondered if Tom might be there.

Chapter Ten

April

Leonora

Since the throwing of the plant plot incident, Leonora hadn't seen Bob. After he'd driven away, she'd gone through a stage of crying and not being able to stop again, and then a return of that incredible anger and then yet more crying.

She wondered whether she'd ever feel whole and found herself buying every women's magazine she could think of to see how other women coped, and what advice she could make use of. None of these helped her and neither did it help when she scoured the internet for the same kind of support.

All this made her feel even more depressed and stuck in an overpowering circle of rage and despair. She had to find a way to survive, but first of all she had to apologise to Bob. It was the right thing to do.

So on Saturday morning, bright and early, Leonora was up and dressed, and trying to prepare herself for the mission she had decided to carry out. She knew from Dorothea where Bob and *that woman* were living. This was in fact *that woman's* home in a town about thirty miles away from where Leonora lived. She still couldn't bring herself to speak the dreaded name out loud, not even in her own mind. She wasn't ready for that yet, and didn't know if she ever would be.

Dorothea had also told her what Bob's plans were this weekend. Admittedly, this was after a fair amount of persuasion on the phone a couple of days ago and presumably because her friend still felt guilty because of what her brother had done. Leonora wasn't proud of how insistent she'd been, but she'd had no choice. Dorothea had told her *that woman* would be out on Saturday morning at the local beauty salon. So the coast would be clear for Leonora to apologise in person to her husband and then leave before *that woman* returned.

Dorothea had said she was happy to warn Bob that Leonora was planning to visit, but Leonora had been horrified at the thought. She'd sworn her friend to secrecy on pain of death, or worse.

So, today, she would drive to her husband's new home, get there around 10.30am – by which time *that woman* would be fully immersed in whatever pointless beauty treatments she was having and therefore safely out of the picture – and then Leonora would have her say and leave. She hoped her actions would be enough to clear the air, and at least they would salve her conscience.

Before she got into the car, Leonora put on her lipstick. She didn't usually bother with it at a weekend, but today was different. Lipstick gave her an extra boost of confidence which she needed. She checked her phone for the directions she'd keyed in the night before, popped it in place on the dashboard and set off. She wondered about some soothing music to calm her nerves as she drove – something like Classic FM that wouldn't be too intrusive – but decided against it. She'd only panic about missing the route if the radio was on and, besides, she was more than fine with driving in silence. It was Bob who had been keen on the radio. Not classical music, but something more contemporary which never seemed to have any tunes. Not that Leonora had ever complained. She'd learnt to suffer in silence.

Perhaps that might have been part of the problem with her marriage …

This unexpected thought made Leonora gasp, and her fingers tightened their grip on the steering wheel for a moment or two. Was her own silence really part of the reason her marriage had broken down? Because she *did* keep the peace on many occasions when she should have been speaking out. Did this mean that Bob had started to take her for granted, which was why he'd looked elsewhere?

No. Of course not, Leonora told herself. The reason for her marriage break-up was entirely and only because Bob had been having an affair with *that woman*. If he hadn't been unfaithful to Leonora, they would still be together. Or at least she assumed they would.

To her surprise, Leonora found she couldn't solve that puzzle. Not to her satisfaction. No matter how many times she approached the issue from a plethora of different angles during her drive, and no matter how many houses and streets and shops whizzed by. However, that wasn't the most annoying thing about her journey.

The most annoying thing was this: there was a *tiny* – and *very* reluctant indeed to announce itself – part of Leonora which couldn't help thinking that suffering in silence was what *that woman* would never ever dream of doing.

Because of this, by the time her sat-nav congratulated her in very condescending tones for the miracle of reaching her destination, Leonora was more frazzled than she'd hoped to be. She'd hoped to arrive at Bob's new home in a cool, calm and collected state. But instead, she felt hot and bothered, and she hoped this wasn't the onset of another hot flush. Looking like a tomato was the last thing she wanted.

To try to distract herself, she switched on the fan to high. Then she found somewhere to park that was far enough away from Bob's house so he wouldn't spot her if he happened to glance outside, and looked around the road to see what the area was like. It gave her an illicit thrill to realise that her estranged husband's new home was less posh than the one he'd left. There was a distinct air of being down-at-heel or of the people who lived here not caring too much about their environment. Some of the front gardens were rather messy and Leonora could even see one with several black bags of rubbish stuffed into one corner. They looked as if they'd been there for a while. That said, they certainly weren't all like that, and Leonora could also see quite a few gardens which were well kept, with one or two pots of spring flowers at the doors.

The houses themselves were fairly old, but classic in design, with bay windows downstairs, in what were presumably living rooms. She'd always fancied the idea of a bay window, but had never in fact lived anywhere with one. One day, maybe.

Anyway, such idle thoughts weren't helping Leonora with her mission. She took a long and steadying breath before checking her make-up and lipstick in the rear-view mirror. She told herself she simply needed to apologise to Bob for her behaviour and then she could return home with the satisfaction of a necessary task completed. She'd pop into Waitrose on the way home and buy a cupcake or brownie for lunch. A treat for herself.

Still practising her apology speech in her head, Leonora got out of her car, locked it, and checked the address for the number of the house (which of course she'd checked about a hundred times last night and about fifty times this morning). Then she began to make her way to Bob's new home.

A couple of minutes later and she was outside the house in question. She knew she was being judgemental, but she couldn't help her surprise that it was one of the better ones in the street. The windows looked new and the front garden was neat, though it didn't have any flowers. Just a paved pathway with freshly-mown grass on either side. In fact, it almost had a welcoming feel about it, though being welcomed was the furthest thing from Leonora's mind.

She squared her shoulders, took another calming breath and pressed the doorbell firmly. She heard the tuneful ring of the bell echoing inside the house and then the sound of approaching footsteps.

Leonora was just in the process of realising that the footsteps weren't Bob's heavy tread when the front door was pulled open and she came face to face with *that woman*.

She dropped her handbag with the shock of it. Her lipstick fell out and rolled into the grass.

"I didn't expect … I mean I thought … you're supposed to be out!" she said, all at once and trying to catch her breath at the same time.

"What the bloody hell are you doing here?" *that woman* replied, her eyes glinting with fury. *"And who the hell gave you our address?"*

"What's going on, Bel?" Leonora heard her husband's voice and then the soft thud of his approaching footsteps in the hallway – the sound she'd been expecting to hear. "Is everything all right? Ah …"

Bob stopped speaking abruptly as he appeared behind the woman he was calling Bel and caught sight of Leonora.

"Ah," he said again as he put a protective arm around *that woman*. "Leonora."

Leonora blinked rapidly and stared at Bob. Her heart was pounding and she absolutely couldn't look at *that woman*. Not now, and possibly not ever. She wished she hadn't come, she wished she hadn't seen what was really happening and she wished she was a thousand miles away from this unexpected and terrible truth.

She stepped back a few paces. Still blinking, she hunkered down and, with hands that refused to stop shaking, picked up her handbag and retrieved her lipstick. Then she straightened up.

"I came here, Bob, to tell you I was sorry for what happened at home when we last saw each other," she said, her voice far gruffer than usual. "But today, having seen what I've seen now, I find I'm not sorry. No, I'm not sorry at all, you cowardly *bastard*."

Then she turned and walked away, the blood still pounding in her ears and her handbag clutched to her stomach like a shield.

Leonora managed to walk like this all the way to the car. She even managed to start the ignition and drive off, though her whole being was numb.

Two streets away, she knew she had to stop and so she pulled over to park in the nearest and easiest space she could see. She turned off the car. She checked to ensure nobody was walking by who might be able to see her. Then she leant her head on the steering wheel and let the tears come. Because all she could see in her head was the image of that woman standing on her doorstep, glowing with health and with her hands on her gently rounded stomach.

Belinda – *that woman* – was pregnant.

*****

Leonora and Bob had never wanted children. It was something they'd talked about early on in their relationship and had discussed again later when things got serious and more committed between them. Leonora had never seen herself as a mother, and had never been very interested in other people's babies. Perhaps this was part of the reason she'd ended up being such close friends with Selena and Dorothea – as they didn't have any maternal feelings either. It was something they'd all laughed about together.

She didn't much feel like laughing now.

She'd taken for granted for so long that Bob didn't want children that even after he'd left Leonora for *that woman*, she'd never once thought about the possibility of her husband becoming a father because of his new life. No, she'd never once imagined that.

Leonora had assumed she was fighting for her marriage alone and not taking a new family into account. She could never compete in that arena. She'd never wanted to, and it was far too late now. Had this been a mistake and had Bob actually wanted children all along?

No, she was sure the decision made so many years ago had been a joint one. They definitely hadn't wanted to be parents. Back then, there'd been too many other things taking their attention away from the vague idea of starting a family: their careers, nights out together, exotic holidays, and so on. This had been their main focus when they'd been newly married and for years afterwards. Leonora had assumed that being happily child-free was stitched into the fabric of their lives together. Now that fabric had been ripped apart by what she'd seen on Bob's doorstep and she wondered if everything she'd ever thought she knew had been a lie.

All these thoughts were still chasing themselves around Leonora's head when she grabbed a table at the pub at the next Friday night catch-up with her friends. She hadn't told either of them yet what she'd discovered, but Dorothea had to know. She must do, as Leonora knew her friend had been seeing Bob – he was her brother after all, so of course she'd been seeing him, or at the very least was in regular contact with him. Leonora also suspected she must know about *that woman* being pregnant. Surely Bob would have told his sister such a vital fact.

The realisation that Dorothea must know this terrible truth but hadn't told her friend made Leonora feel sick. But this time, she didn't feel angry. She didn't feel as if she never wanted to see or speak to Dotts again. Not as she had when she'd first discovered Bob's affair. This time Leonora felt incredibly sad about just how complicated it was all turning out to be, but she also understood how Dotts would see the pregnancy as not something she herself could tell Leonora. Dotts would have wanted Bob to tell her the facts.

Dotts would have been trying to persuade her brother to tell the truth to his wife.

Yes, Leonora understood this as if the words were written in her blood. In her heart, she knew she could trust the quality of Dotts' friendship. She felt the same about Selena. These truths were deep and they were precious.

But Bob hadn't bothered to tell her the truth. He'd not mentioned anything when they'd met up in the bar and certainly not when he'd come round to get his belongings. Yes, that last encounter had ended with Leonora throwing things at him but, even so, it was surely his responsibility to tell her his bit on the side was pregnant.

If Leonora was angry with anyone, she was angry with Bob. Yes, Bob. That *bloody* man. She didn't think she'd been angry with her husband about what he'd done before now. She'd been furious with him on occasions, but not properly angry. She'd been angry with everyone around him: *that woman*, Dotts, and even herself. Yes, she'd been angry with herself for failing to keep her marriage on track and for failing to have the kind of happy life she'd thought she would have.

But Bob? No, she'd not been truly angry with him. Not until now. Once she came to look at it – really look at it – Leonora could see perfectly well how it was all the fault of her bloody husband. He was the one who'd chosen to have an affair and throw away his marriage. He was the one who'd made that woman pregnant – *Belinda*, her name was *Belinda* and perhaps it was time Leonora started to use her name instead of making her into the witch she might not actually be – and he was also the one who'd not told her about his unborn child.

The utter bastard! How dare Bob go around upsetting everyone and turning their lives upside down, whilst he simply swanned along doing whatever he damn well wanted. How dare he! Leonora wished she'd thrown something far bigger at her husband's car when he'd driven away, and that it had caused some real damage.

Not actual injury of course. She wasn't insane. But something painful enough so that Bob would give his selfish decisions more than a second's thought before he made them. Yes, that would be an improvement for sure.

"Hey! You're here first!" Selena's voice carried across the floor with all the enthusiasm of a tide of holidaymakers finally catching sight of the sea. "Good for you!"

Leonora looked round to see both Selena and Dotts making their way past the tables to get to the one she'd chosen. Selena was dressed in something vibrant and orange with a purple scarf and earrings, and Dotts was in her usual dark grey work suit. Though it did look a little less put together than usual. Had Dotts had a bad week too? Well, it couldn't be any worse than Leonora's, that was certain.

After a quick round of hugs and greetings, Selena and Dotts settled themselves in while Leonora went to the bar and ordered a bottle of white and three glasses. She recognised the barman from before. He was the one who'd been sweet on Dotts, or so Selena had insisted. He nodded at her and glanced behind her shoulder.

"Are you here with your friends?" he asked.

"Yes. We're at the table in the corner, the one just down the two steps," Leonora replied as she retrieved her card for payment.

"Then no need to wait, ma'am," he said. "I'll bring it over to you."

"Oh, okay," she said. "That's very kind."

Leonora returned to the table, pushing gently through the Friday night pub crowd. As she approached, her friends both looked up with a smile, but Selena's expression quickly turned to puzzlement.

"What? Have they run out of wine?"

Leonora had to laugh. "What a horrific idea! No, I've put our order in, and the barman said he'd bring it over to us in a minute."

"Ah," Selena's frown cleared. "Is this the same barman who has a soft spot for Dotts?"

"Don't be ridiculous," Dotts began to protest but the sudden rush of colour to her cheeks told a different story.

Leonora was sure Selena was about to launch into more teasing of poor Dorothea. However, at that exact moment, the man himself appeared with the wine bottle and three glasses.

"Evening," he said and glanced first at all of them before his gaze rested on Dorothea. "How are things with you? I mean *really*?"

Leonora was sure that, even though his question appeared to be for everyone, he was talking to Dotts alone. He was certainly only looking at her.

"We're all right, thank you," Dorothea replied. "We're muddling through, and we've got a lot to talk about tonight, but thank you."

"My pleasure, ma'am," the barman replied and then nodded at them. "Let me know if you need anything else, and enjoy your evening."

With that he was gone. Leonora smiled to herself as she poured the wine, but Selena was already laughing.

"He really likes you, doesn't he!" her friend said to Dotts. "You should find out his name for sure. He's so up for a date with you, Dotty!"

Dorothea tried to quell Selena with a look, but Leonora knew from experience this was highly unlikely to work. Selena was such a romantic at heart and had been hoping to find someone for Dotts ever since they'd been friends.

"Or maybe I should go and ask him his name!" Selena continued. "I could get his number for you?"

Dorothea groaned. "No! Anyway, I already know his name. He's called Tom. He left his job in Australia last year and is working his way round Europe in the way he always wanted to."

There was a second or two of utter silence at the table before Selena opened her mouth and came out with a barrage of questions.

"What? How do you know all this? When did this happen? *Are you actually going out together?*"

"No, we are not," Dorothea protested. "Something happened recently at work which I need to tell you about and I ended up here on a Monday evening for a quick drink before I went home. Tom was working that night and he was kind enough to listen to me. That's all."

Dotty paused, and Leonora thought she might be about to add something else. But her friend simply shook her head as if dislodging a thought or two, and stayed silent.

Leonora leaned forward and took hold of Dorothea's hand.

"What happened at work?" she asked.

Dorothea blinked and then straightened her shoulders.

"There's a new restructuring programme in the office," she said. "Which means my team and I are in line for redundancy. I meant to text you both to let you know but I didn't know what to type."

"Oh, honey," Selena said, putting her arm round Dotty's shoulders. "I'm so very sorry. You'll be okay, won't you? I mean you've been there for ages. You have a vast amount of experience. You know so much."

Dorothea shook her head. "I'm not sure that means anything these days. It's all about the money now. Our team doesn't bring in a lot of profit – it's not what we were set up to do. We're there to provide advice to UK businesses so *they* can make more profit. We're not there to make money ourselves. At least, that's what I thought."

Leonora listened with all her sympathies in play as she knew how much her job meant to Dorothea. She was so sorry her friend was having to go through this, and at such a difficult time of life too. Nobody wanted to employ women in their late fifties. It was so hard to start again at that age. She hoped it would be okay for Dotts, and she could keep her job. At the same time, she couldn't help admitting it was something of a relief from her own worries. Not that she wanted either of her good friends to be unhappy about anything. Perish that terrible thought. But it stopped her obsessing about herself and her pesky husband, and that at least had to be a positive thing.

Finally, Dorothea came to the end of her story.

"I don't know what to do," she sighed. "Though I suppose there's nothing I can do. Not at this stage. And that makes me feel so helpless, which I can't help hating."

Selena hugged Dotts even harder. "Isn't there something your work can do? I mean, what with …"

Dorothea sat up and looked straight at Selena. "What with … *what?*"

Selena stopped hugging her and sat back on her chair. "Well, you *know*. With your *actual* job and everything …"

Another beat of silence and then Dorothea rolled her eyes.

"Oh honestly, Selena. You do realise that all that spy fantasy nonsense has always been just in your own head, don't you? And, yes, I know I've not said anything in the past because I thought it was funny and perhaps I *should* have said something, but I wanted to sound less dull. The truth is I'm nothing more than a civil service administrator, in business support, and though it's ordinary compared to what you do, I've always loved it. And now even that might be taken away, and I don't know what to think. But, really and truly, I'm not a spy, I've never been a spy and I don't know anyone who is a spy."

This was the longest speech Dorothea had given for as far back as Leonora could remember. In addition, she couldn't recall her friend ever sounding as impassioned about anything.

Selena stared at Dorothea and swallowed. She looked as serious as Leonora had ever seen her. "I'm sorry I made you feel like you were ordinary in any way, Dotty. That's the last thing I'd ever want you to feel. I got carried away, and I'm sorry. But I'm not sorry to have you as a friend. Because you're the kindest and most caring person I know, and I couldn't ever imagine not being friends with you. And that makes you extraordinary in every way, in my opinion."

A beat of silence and then Selena continued. "And you're not so bad either, Leonora, but obviously not as lovely as Dotts. That would be impossible for either of us, don't you think?"

Leonora couldn't help laughing and, in her heart, agreeing Selena was right. There was nothing ordinary about their Dotts. Nothing at all.

The moment was celebrated with another sip or two of wine and, for a while, the three women tried to come up with a plan for what Dorothea might be able to do. In the end, they had to admit their friend's job situation was pretty much a waiting game and Leonora thought, not for the first time, how annoying it was that the management in any office always had the power on their side. Still, there was some comfort in knowing Dotts had been in her job for such a long time that the redundancy money, whether enhanced or not, would be more than enough to keep her going for at least six months, and probably more.

Dorothea hadn't worked out the money angle of it yet, and Leonora gently encouraged her to look at it so she could have all the facts at her fingertips. Just in case.

"But I don't want to leave my job if I can possibly help it," Dotty protested. "I don't want them to think that."

"They won't," Leonora was quick to encourage her. "You can ask HR to give you the figures and it won't affect how they see you and your job role. I'm not even sure HR is allowed to tell the management team you've asked the question, but don't quote me on that. I'm no lawyer. Besides, knowing all the facts and figures does you no harm."

"I agree," Selena said. "I mean I don't have the first idea as to what happens in the corporate business world as I've always been a sole trader. But knowing all the options is surely a good thing."

And Dotty couldn't help but agree with them. Selena drained her wine, took the bottle and replenished their glasses.

"Anyway," said Dotty, sounding tired but somehow relieved. "What's been going on with everyone else? How are things with you, Leonora?"

And there it was. The moment Leonora had been dreading. She put down her wine and took a deep and shuddering breath.

"I've found out that the woman Bob left me for – *Belinda* – is pregnant," she said simply.

A long silence, and then Selena gasped. "Oh shit. That's *awful*."

Dotts reached out and put a gentle hand on Leonora's arm. "Did Bob tell you?"

Leonora shook her head. "No. I drove over to see him at the address you gave me at the time you said Belinda would be out. I was going to apologise for throwing a plant pot at his car as I thought I owed my bloody husband an apology. But it turns out he owes me one instead. Because Belinda hadn't gone out anywhere and she answered the door. So I saw she was pregnant. It was obvious."

"Oh, Leonora," Dotty squeezed her arm more firmly. "I'm so sorry. I've been telling him for ages he absolutely has to tell you and I'm so sorry you found out like this. He's not told me what happened when you went round – I would have said a few choice words if he had."

"You knew this?" Selena cut in, turning to Dotts, her eyes wide. "You knew and you didn't tell poor Leonora?"

This was exactly what Leonora herself had been thinking but her thought processes were further along than Selena's.

"It's not Dotty's fault," Leonora spoke before the situation had a chance to spiral out of hand. "If I'd been in the same position, I wouldn't have known what to do either. It's not Dotty's story to tell, is it? It's Bob's."

"Thank you," Dorothea said. "Thank you."

Selena, however, snorted and gave Dotty a sidelong glance. "Well, I think you're being very generous, Leonora. Dotty – you're our friend, you know! Surely Leonora needed some kind of warning? But never mind all that now. Leonora – how are you coping with this?"

And that of course was the million-dollar question. Leonora had no idea how she was coping. Ever since she'd found out about the pregnancy, she'd been on yet another rollercoaster ride between an almost overwhelming fury and an equally powerful grief. As she clutched her wine glass like a security blanket, she tried to explain some of this to her closest friends.

"I don't know," she said quietly as Selena and Dotty listened to her. "I was shocked of course. I still am. I don't now know if Bob left me because that woman was pregnant and he felt he 'had to do the right thing' or something stupid like that. Or if he left me because he was so thrilled to find out he was going to be a father. All my married life, I've believed Bob and I were happy – more than happy – being childless, but now I wonder if that was a lie all along. For him at least. When he left, I thought what I had to do was fight Belinda to get him back – and I wanted him back, so much! But now I see I was fighting against a whole new life and a family, and there's nothing I can offer Bob to match it, if that's what he truly wants."

With that, Leonora started to cry again. Even though she'd thought her tears were over and there were no more inside, she was wrong. As she cried, her two friends tried to comfort her, more wine was called for, and the evening became far more of a support session than it usually was. But, then again, these were her friends and it had been a rough week and who else now could she turn to?

Whatever happened, Leonora knew she was lucky to have these two women in her life. When the crying was over and she felt calmer, she was so glad she'd come out to see them tonight. They were both, in different ways, her rock.

At the end of the night, it was Selena who gave Leonora and Dotty something positive to consider. Which they definitely needed. After the wine bill was paid, and after Dotty had had what looked to be a short but intense conversation with the barman, Selena turned to them and smiled.

"I know it's been a tricky night for you two," she said. "So I thought I'd give you something positive to hang on to. Would you like to come to the press night of the play I'm doing the costumes for? Please say yes!"

Chapter Eleven

April

Selena

Dating wasn't something Selena had ever expected she'd be doing. Yes, she liked sex and was more than happy to have a brief fling with an attractive and available man if one happened to pass by and notice her. But she'd always assumed she and the man in question would drift apart and move on.

It wasn't like this with Max. In fact, Selena was enjoying herself more than she'd ever done in the past. As a result, her stitching was more magical, and the costumes she and the twins were making for the actors seemed to fit perfectly first time and be absolutely what the play had been crying out for all along. According to Grant.

This miracle was affecting everything she did, and everything the twins helped her with too. Sometimes she wondered if the two girls could actually see the colours that had only ever been visible to her, but she hadn't asked them. They were such a mysterious pair and Selena was a great believer in not delving too much into any mystery. The universe should be allowed to keep its secrets – it was part of the way it worked. Not only that, but there was a magic and a mystery about twins that Selena was happy to experience but reluctant to try to explain.

That said, she wasn't sure Max would agree. He was a man of curiosity and liked to understand things in order to appreciate them fully. Not that this worried her. Their differences made the colours dance and sparkle more brightly.

Selena was, in effect, supremely happy. For the moment. Because of course she knew it wouldn't last. Max would one day soon return to the States and she would need to try to be prepared. This difficult future wasn't something she liked to think about, so she was concentrating instead on her current happiness. It was an emotion she was very much enjoying although she couldn't help feeling guilty on her friends' behalf. Both of them. However, her heart couldn't help dancing at the thought of seeing Max this afternoon. It was Saturday and they'd finally got round to choosing a time for Selena to show him the parts of London she loved, just as he'd taken her to the bar he loved on their first date.

Today, she and Max had agreed to meet at Charing Cross station. Selena arrived at the designated meeting point about five minutes early as she didn't want to look too keen, but was pleased to see Max was already there. He was leaning against a wall, intent on his phone, but something must have made him sense her arrival as he looked up and gave her a wide smile.

"Selena! You're early."

"Not as early as you," she replied as they exchanged a brief kiss and hug. "But I never like being late. How did you know I was here?"

"What do you mean?" Max asked as he linked her arm with his and they began to walk along together. "I always know when you're there. Of course I do!"

"What a smoothie!" Selena replied with a smile. "But it can't be true. There are loads of people milling around. It's a nice Saturday afternoon in London. What I mean is you looked up as I approached. Coincidence or did something tell you I was there?"

She was teasing him and didn't expect Max to answer seriously but, once again, he surprised her.

"You know, you're right," he said, pulling her closer to him. "I did know you were there when I looked up. And I think I've known that before too. There's just something about you, Selena, that I must be aware of. As if there's an aura you carry which I'm sensitive to. No idea if that makes any sense and you can blame it on the theatre and the play taking over my brain, but that's the nearest I can get to describing it."

There at the edge of the station just before reaching The Strand, Selena stopped walking and turned to face Max. A couple of people behind muttered something and had to sidestep them to avoid a collision, but she didn't care about that.

"Honestly," she said softly so he had to lean forward to hear her. "Honestly, that's the most romantic thing anyone has ever said to me. Thank you."

And then she kissed him, properly this time. Even though they were in a public place. As the colours between them fizzed and sparkled at the contact, Selena realised this was the first time anyone she knew had spoken about an aura. People didn't believe in such things and tended only to mention auras when they were joking. Max had been serious. She wondered whether one day she might find the courage to tell him about the colours she saw and what they meant to her.

Though she must remember he wouldn't stay for ever and the opportunity was unlikely to arise. She told herself simply to enjoy the here and now. With him. So, once they had finished their kiss, Selena was happy to walk along a bright and busy London street in the spring sunshine and count her colours. Not that she turned out to have much time for idleness as Max started to laugh.

"What?" she said, feeling his laughter stir up the brightness in her heart. "What have I said?"

"Nothing," he was quick to reassure her. "Nothing bad. But I'm curious to know where we're walking to. If anywhere. Though I'm happy to walk round the whole of London with you, if that's your plan."

"Good to know," Selena replied. "But I have other ideas. I've decided we're going to have a wander round a couple of my favourite galleries. As long as you're happy with art?"

"Sounds good to me," Max replied. "Will it be fabric and costumes?"

His assumption made sense, but Selena wasn't intending to do that. She preferred to visit such magical places herself, as the colours could be very powerful as they mingled and danced with her own.

"A good guess," she replied. "But you don't want to spend all afternoon watching me drool over fabric – and yes that would happen – so I've decided today is a day for paintings. And coffee and cake. You can't admire art without food. It's simply not possible."

"Sounds good," Max said. "So where are we heading?"

She told him as they continued to walk in the direction she wanted to go. Her plan for this afternoon was to spend some time at the National Portrait Gallery, only recently reopened after its long refit. Then, if there was time, they would take a brisk walk round the larger and far better-known National Gallery. Both galleries were very close to Charing Cross, which was why Selena had chosen the meeting point.

"A National Portrait Gallery?" Max said. "I've honestly never heard of it."

Selena sighed. "I know! Nobody has, and it's not helped that they've been closed for quite a while lately. I keep on singing their praises and encouraging everyone to visit at least once – well, when they're open. But honestly, it's one of London's hidden treasures. Here we are."

To Selena's surprise, when they came round the corner, there was a small queue waiting to get in. This had never happened before. Indeed, on some visits, she'd been almost the only person there, especially if she'd gone at opening time.

"Goodness," she said. "This is definitely not what I was expecting."

"But it's Saturday afternoon at the start of the tourist season," Max pointed out. "Isn't this primetime visiting hours?"

She had to admit he had a point and gave a wry shrug. "I think you overstate the urge of the London tourist to spend an hour or two looking at portraits."

Max gave a mock gasp and winked at her. "But I thought all London tourists were desperate for some culture, and this is why they visit your capital city in the first place. Well, that and the theatre of course. It's world-class."

Selena smiled at him.

"And I thought everyone came here for the royal family!" she said.

"Oh, that as well. Naturally."

They didn't have to wait long, and ten minutes later they were inside, the security guards having assessed Selena's handbag as harmless. She couldn't remember anyone checking it last time but, of course, it had been over a year since she'd visited.

Inside, everything had changed. No more the small dark hallway and passage towards the ticket desk. Instead, everything was larger and lighter. The ticket area was no longer at the front so the hallway itself seemed to have doubled in size and the carvings on the walls and ceiling were far more on show.

"Well," Selena said, gazing upward and around. "This is different."

"Different good, or different bad?" Max asked her.

"Different good. I mean look at these carvings. And the light! Though maybe …"

"Maybe …?"

"Maybe it's lost something. It's not as cosy as it used to be. At least not on my first impression. Though I hope they've kept some of the cosiness in the rooms. That's always been part of its charm."

Max laughed. "I don't think I've ever heard of a gallery aiming to be cosy. This is going to be an eye-opening experience, that's for sure."

And it was.

Selena and Max wandered round the newly-reopened gallery for a good hour or two, simply taking in the pictures and photographs on display. Selena liked to enter a room, pick one picture – or at the most two – that particularly called to her and spend some time in front of it, letting the colours and patterns speak. Max had a different approach. He preferred to give each exhibit some time and then return to the one he had liked the most. Selena understood that all too well, but she'd quickly learned how too much colour input muddled her responses and made everything more confusing. It was best for her to focus on her chosen pictures and ignore the rest.

At first, Selena felt disorientated – the new look in the gallery was certainly less intimate than it had once been. She'd always loved the feeling of being in the home of someone she might know and admiring their art collection. Now, it was more like a public gallery and there were many more visitors than she'd ever known. This made it more challenging to choose a picture and then admire it.

Several times, Selena was forced to move away and come back after a little while to pick up her contemplation where she'd left it.

Not that she should be complaining. Of course she shouldn't! After Covid, every single museum and gallery in the country had been struggling. If these changes brought in more visitors and therefore more income, that could only be a good thing. Selena knew this perfectly well, but she couldn't help thinking something had been lost. Something that might not ever return.

All that said and thought, the pictures themselves were the heart of the matter. As they always would be. As she and Max continued their gentle exploration of the gallery together, Selena realised that the place itself wasn't the only thing to have changed. She'd changed too. The most significant and obvious change was that she wasn't here on her own. It was – now she came to think of it – the first time she'd ever visited this gallery with someone else. She'd never brought Leonora or Dorothea here. She'd never even considered it. Walking around galleries and taking in the beauty found inside was not their cup of tea. Or indeed coffee.

It was strange that Max should be the very first person to accompany her. And whilst she thought more deeply about that,

Selena could see how much she'd changed in her tastes and understanding of art too.

Just ten or so years ago, for instance, her first love would have been the older portraits in the gallery which made her think of past people and the stories they'd known. She could imagine their personalities and their lives, and it made her think of her own.

Now, she preferred the newer portraits and the energy they contained. She liked recognising people from television and from theatre, and seeing how the picture changed the way she thought about them. Because the portrait of someone known always did change the way she thought about them or deepen the impression she already had. Either way, this was a change. In herself.

These thoughts filled her mind with a soft swoop of colour – yellow and cream, wild green and a gentle blue – and she shook her head to allow the patterns to free themselves.

"Everything okay?" Max's voice brought her back into the present, and she smiled up at him.

"Yes, I think so," she said. "Just taking it all in. And I think it's probably time for coffee, don't you agree?"

The enthusiasm with which her companion greeted her suggestion made her smile for two reasons. The first was she didn't know anyone who didn't respond to an invitation for coffee with anything less than total enthusiasm. And the second reason was that, no matter how much anyone including herself enjoyed admiring art, one always needed a refreshment break at regular intervals.

However, the quiet and comforting café Selena had been looking forward to was, sadly, no more. Instead they ended up in the brand-new café which was situated in a long and very brightly-lit corridor. Not only that but they had to queue up in a very awkward manner and Selena found the menu near the door hard to read. It was typed in the kind of script that made her head ache. Her annoyance made Max smile and he was kind enough to read it out to her – at least the important items which were the type of coffee on offer and what the cakes might be – though his very kindness did make her feel rather older than she wished to admit to.

This thought made her giggle and her headache at once eased.

"What is it?" Max asked, still peering at the menu and chanting what he thought might be appropriate for her to know. "Have I pronounced something wrong? You have to give us Americans some leeway, you know – it's lucky we can read at all."

This just made Selena laugh even more. "No, it's not that! It's just that this whole thing has aged me at least twenty years. This new café is meant only for the young."

"Or those who can work out the curly typeface," Max added, and Selena had to agree.

By the time they finally reached the counter, she was desperate for her coffee, but was once again rather put-out to see that the available cakes had been reduced in size by at least half from what they had been when she was last here. This, she supposed, was what counted for progress these days: the produce got smaller, but the price got larger.

Oh well. She shouldn't complain as she knew how much the gallery needed the money. But she couldn't help feeling disheartened by the time they managed to grab a (very small) table at the far end of the space. And they'd only managed that as the family who'd been there just before were leaving as she and Max approached.

Once settled in and with their trays unpacked, Selena looked at the people around them and grimaced.

"Sorry about all this," she said to Max.

"Sorry? Why?"

She sighed. "Because it's not how I was expecting it to be. The old café was tucked away in the basement and was utterly quirky in every way. All higgledy-piggledy and with seats that you could never quite fit into, but it was filled with more pictures and bookshelves, and it had a warm and friendly feel. The staff were always lovely too. This is just so ... so ... impersonal. And bleak."

"But it's clean and the coffee is good," Max pointed out. "So it's not all bad. And besides, I have nothing to compare it with and it seems like a perfectly reasonable little diner to me."

Selena nodded and thought about that for a moment before taking a cautious sip of her coffee. Max was right. It *was* good. That at least was positive.

"And in addition," Max continued, "I've just spent an enjoyable hour or so looking at pictures I never expected to see with a woman I really like and never expected to meet. So having coffee and a snack in a place where there's nothing else of interest to look at so I can concentrate entirely on her is a plus point as far as I'm concerned."

Selena stared at him, caught the twinkle in his eye and groaned. "You're such a smoothie. Just shut up and drink your coffee!"

They smiled at each other and Selena admired once more the way their individual colours sparked and danced between them. That private joy made her think though and, after a moment or two, Max touched her hand.

"Is anything wrong?" he asked.

"No," she said slowly, putting down her coffee cup. "Not wrong exactly. I was just thinking how lucky I feel. Meeting you, I mean, and the way the rehearsals and the costumes are coming along. I thought at the start of this year that it would be an ordinary one. Not bad. Not at all. Ordinary doesn't have to be a bad thing. I was expecting things to carry on much as they have in the past. In a good way. But everything with Leonora and Dotty has been so awful lately and it seems they can't find a way out of the terrible things happening to them. I feel guilty that Leonora's having to cope with such a nightmare break-up, and poor Dotty is facing the loss of a job she's loved for ever. And here I am loving spending time with you, Max, and in a job I love as well. It's not fair, is it? It's not fair at all."

Selena felt the tears threatening to fall. And for more reasons that she'd been able to admit. So she fell silent and instead took a sip of that extraordinarily good coffee in an attempt to revive herself and stop being such a wet blanket. This seemed to help, as did the warmth of Max's hand on hers. She'd already told him the basic facts about her two friends. Of course, she'd been running for a train to get to Leonora's when she and Max first met, so he was somehow already involved in that particular drama, although at a distance. He was up to speed about poor Dotty too.

"I know you're worried about your friends," Max's voice eased its way through the frightening colours whirling through Selena's mind. "Of course you are. But what's happened to them isn't your fault, Selena. It's not that you enjoying life can ever make things worse for them. That's not how the world works. But what you *are* doing is showing how much you care, and trying to do everything in your power to help them. That's all you can do. It's the most important thing."

Selena nodded and gave him half a smile. She knew he was right. And she was grateful for his words. But she still wished everything would be good for her friends again.

"Thank you," she said. "You're right, I know. I'm just hoping the rest of the year will be much better for them than the start of it has been."

"I'll drink to that," Max said, and the two of them clinked their coffee cups together and smiled.

After coffee, they decided to look again at the more modern portraits in the gallery. Max commented that this area was more to his taste, and the colours of his aura certainly deepened and sparkled more brightly as they wandered round. He was especially interested in the portraits of actors, exclaiming with delight when he saw the painting of Judi Dench and waxing very lyrical indeed about her work.

"She's astonishing!" he said, gazing in awe at her portrait in a way that might have made Selena ever so slightly jealous if she'd been that kind of woman. Which she most definitely was not. "Every play or movie she's in just glitters. She's such a huge talent."

Selena couldn't help but agree, and Max's enthusiasm made her smile too. Not least because his American accent became a thousand times stronger when he was excited about something.

After they'd had enough of the portraits on offer, they made their way to the National Gallery just round the corner. There was still something of a queue here but Selena reckoned it was worth their while even for a short visit. The building was as always utterly stunning in every way. Whenever she walked inside, no matter how busy or how loud the foyer was, the colours inside her started to sing.

Max was impressed too.

"Wow," he breathed. "Wow. *This building.* We have nothing like this in the States. Nothing at all. And it's *free?*"

"Yes, totally free," Selena replied. "Though of course there are plenty of places to leave your money if you want to give a donation."

"Sounds good," Max replied and immediately found a donation box and pushed in some notes.

Selena laughed. "You're such a tourist!"

"That's true," he said. "I suppose I am. Don't you British people like to donate to buildings as astonishing as this? Shame on you."

"Oh no," Selena shook her head, trying not to smile. "The locals never donate. We feel it's our right *not* to pay for things if we can help it. Haven't you realised that yet?"

"Ah, that explains a lot about the British," Max said.

And she supposed it did.

They didn't stay long in the National Gallery. Max seemed more taken with the building itself than the glorious artwork on offer, but Selena didn't mind. It was enough that she could see how much he was enjoying himself. That in itself made her feel happy in a way she couldn't remember feeling happy before. Not about any other man she'd ever known. She was coming to realise Max was special, but once more she told herself to be practical. There could be no future. Not really. But that didn't mean she couldn't enjoy his company today.

Outside the gallery, they walked slowly, hand in hand, towards the tube station. They hadn't made any arrangements about the evening though Selena knew they would go either to his or her home to be together. There was something she didn't quite know, however. Something all the colours in her heart were pushing her to ask.

"So," she said, rolling the thoughts through her head. "So, did you enjoy visiting this very small part of the London I know and love?"

Max stopped walking and pulled her gently to the side of the pavement so they didn't disturb anyone else.

"Yes," he said. "I did. Very much. You have such beautiful artwork in your country and such wonderful buildings. Thank you very much for a very enjoyable time. But, to be honest, I would have enjoyed spending the afternoon with you wherever you took me. As I said earlier on. I really do like you, Selena."

And then he kissed her. And, for that moment in time, it was as if she and Max were the only two people in the whole world. She kissed him back, and the colours flowed between them in the kind of perfect rainbow she could only marvel at.

The kiss might have lasted forever or for only a few moments. She couldn't tell. But when it was over, Selena stepped back a pace and gazed up at him.

"Come to mine tonight," she said quietly. "And this time, stay over. This time, I don't want to wake up without you."

"I thought you'd never ask," he said.

Chapter Twelve

Dorothea

April

Dorothea had had quite enough of her brother. She was of course pleased that the secret about Belinda's pregnancy was out in the open and she didn't have to worry about how Leonora would react or the inevitable pain it would cause her. But she couldn't approve of the way poor Leonora had found out.

That said, her feckless brother wasn't the only aspect of the year making her cross. She was also cross that she herself had been weak enough to give Bob's new address to Leonora and advise her that the Saturday they'd pinpointed together would be a good time to catch him alone. She was therefore partly to blame for Leonora's continuing unhappiness.

So, this morning, the last Sunday in April, she'd told Bob she would expect him at her house at 3pm for tea and a very important talk. She'd added there was no option for refusal and he should come on his own. Because what she wanted to say to her brother was not for Belinda's ears.

It was now 2.55pm and Dorothea had switched on the kettle. She would make the tea as soon as Bob arrived and they would take it and the biscuits she'd purchased yesterday into her living room. It was probably nice enough to sit in the garden, but she didn't want the neighbours to overhear. She wanted her words to be for her brother alone. At her feet, Oscar swirled around, his soft white fur undulating with the movement, and she bent down to stroke him.

Oscar gazed up at her solemnly, blinked a couple of times and then wandered off, presumably realising she wasn't going to be refilling his food bowl right now.

The sound of the doorbell pierced through the rising growl of the kettle, making her jump. She'd not heard Bob's car arriving. She'd been too deep in thought. Or worry.

Leaving the kettle to finish boiling, Dorothea made her way to the front door, trying to breathe calmly and remember the purpose of this meeting. On the threshold, Bob was smiling far too brightly and clutching a bunch of sorry-looking flowers to his chest. Clearly purchased at the local garage. He must be feeling guilty as he'd never bought her flowers before. But, then again, he had an awful lot to feel guilty about.

Dorothea grimaced. She took the flowers with nothing more than a brief nod, and stepped aside to let him in.

Bob took off his jacket, still wearing that ridiculous smile, and rubbed his hands together. Even though it wasn't cold.

"So! Lovely to see you this sunny afternoon, sis," he said. "Though you didn't really invite me, did you? It was more of an order."

Dorothea shot him a sharp glance as she took the meagre floral offering into the kitchen to get a vase. Though, from the look of the flowers, they were probably beyond the ministrations of water.

"Don't call me *sis*," she said. "You know I hate it."

"Oh. Yes. Sorry! My bad."

She hated people who said *my bad* too. It wasn't a proper phrase, for heaven's sake. Something he'd picked up from Belinda, she assumed.

Dorothea dropped the flowers unceremoniously into the first vase she found. She then prepared the tea while Bob continued to fidget around the kitchen. She wished he would be still, but he'd never been one for sitting down and doing nothing. He was unlikely to change now.

"Come on then," she said when the tea was ready. "I'll take this through. You can bring the biscuits. We can talk then."

"Okay," Bob said.

In her living room, Bob put the plate of biscuits down on the coffee table and ambled over to the window.

"Your garden looks lovely," he said. "It's probably warm enough to sit outside if you wanted to."

"Yes, it probably is," Dorothea replied. "But I'm afraid I don't want to. I'd prefer to talk to you in here."

Bob turned and blinked at her and she couldn't blame him. She couldn't remember when she'd sounded quite so determined. She was usually – no, *always* – the woman who fitted in as best she could with the people around her, including her colleagues, her friends and Bob. She had never been the one to suggest anything, let alone demand it.

Perhaps today was the time for something different.

"Okay," Bob said again and sat down in one of her cosy armchairs while Dorothea sat in the one opposite.

She poured the tea and offered Bob a biscuit. He took one and began to nibble at the edges, casting her the occasional worried glance as he did so.

Dorothea took a sip of her tea. Perfect. Just as she liked it. The taste of it gave her the strength she required to tell Bob what needed to be said.

"As you no doubt have realised," she began, "I didn't ask you here today for a social visit."

Her brother raised one eyebrow. "Yes, even I gathered that."

She ignored his sarcasm. She had no time for it. Not today.

"I asked you here," she said, powering on through, "because it's high time you stopped keeping Leonora in the dark with what your plans are and started being honest and open with her. It's utterly unfair and terrible that she had to find out about Belinda's pregnancy in the way she did. Yes, I shouldn't have told her your address and I accept I was at fault there, and I'm sorry. But it was *you* who should have told your wife where you're staying and it was *you* who should have told her about the pregnancy. You can't keep avoiding Leonora and hoping all this disaster will just go away if you ignore it for long enough. Life's not like that, Bob. It's not like that at all, and it's time you grew up and started to take some responsibility for the mess you've created."

For a moment there was utter silence. Then Bob flung his half-nibbled biscuit back on the plate and sprang to his feet. Oscar, who had followed them both in earlier, turned tail and ran into the hallway.

"What on earth gives *you* the right to pass judgement on *me*?" Bob spat at her as he began to pace up and down across the room. "Who the hell do you think you are? I've never judged your life and I've been nothing but supportive of you. I know the situation is difficult and I need to try to sort things out. I'm not an idiot! But I'm trying to let Leonora know these things as gently as I can and not in a way that causes her any more problems. I would have told her about the baby. Of course I would! But at the time I thought was right. Not at a random time chosen by my ruddy sister who didn't give me any warning what she'd done! How do you think Belinda felt when she opened the door and saw Leonora standing there? She wasn't feeling well that day, which was why she cancelled the salon. And finding my estranged wife on her doorstep didn't make things any better, I can tell you! If you'd just left well alone, everything would have worked out better than it has at the moment. Because I know you've invited me here – if *invited* is the word and I'm not sure it is – to give me an ear-bashing. Just like you used to do when we were children. Some things never change. But, in all honesty, Dorothea, everything right now would be a whole lot easier if you just *butted out and left well alone!*"

Bob stopped speaking at last. He spun round, and gave her a furious glare before sitting down in the seat he'd vacated. He picked up his biscuit and stuffed the rest of it into his mouth, still glaring at her.

Dorothea felt exhausted, just listening to him. She also felt extremely annoyed at the injustice of his accusations. She put down her teacup, which was gently shaking in her grasp, and took a much-needed breath.

"It seems to me," she said, surprised beyond measure by how calm she sounded, "that leaving things well alone hasn't brought you or Leonora much luck in the past few months. You've had an affair, split up with your wife, and you're now living with a woman who's having your baby. That doesn't sound much like any kind of easy life to me."

Bob glared at her again. He looked as if he was about to launch into another speech accusing her of all manner of things, so she steeled herself for it. Thankfully it didn't come.

Instead, he pushed one hand through his hair which made it stick up into ridiculous points, and sighed deeply.

"You're right," he said, swallowing hard. "It's not the year I wanted to have. It's not the kind of year I imagined."

Dorothea almost smiled but knew quite well now wasn't the time for smiling. This kind of behaviour was Bob all over. Throughout his whole childhood and teenage years, and well into his twenties too, her brother had got himself into all sorts of trouble with all sorts of people. He was at heart a mischief maker and perhaps he'd never truly grown out of that approach to life. He'd always been in trouble at school, and it was amazing he'd passed his exams so well as he seemed to spend most of his classes messing around at the back. Once he reached his early teens, he'd been more interested in girls than study and had always been the one their parents had worried about most. Even though she was the girl so they should really have been worrying more about her. Bob's mischief had meant she'd had no other role to play in their family set-up apart from the sensible one. Though that was the role she was happiest in, of course. Wasn't it?

"I never meant for any of this to happen," Bob continued, quietly. "But I know what you're saying and I know you mean well. I do need to start making decisions about all this. When I first met Belinda, I was swept up in how I felt about her. I'm not saying I don't love Leonora, because I do. Even though I know none of you believe that anymore. And I can't say I blame you. If I was looking at all this and what's happened from the outside, I wouldn't believe me either. But I've never felt this strongly about anyone as I do about Belinda. She makes me feel alive in a way I don't think I've felt in a long time. Leonora is a wonderful woman – I know that – and I've treated her terribly – I know that too – but somewhere along the line, I just … I just fell *out* of love with her, and I fell *in* love with Belinda. And there's nothing I can do about it. Before Belinda, I didn't think I ever wanted children but, when she told me she was pregnant, I couldn't believe how overjoyed I was with the news. It made sense of everything. It made sense of my life. And I know there are things I have to do about Leonora – things I should have done before – but I think everything is different now."

This was the most her brother had ever said to Dorothea about anything, and she could sense the sincerity behind his words. There was no way back for Bob and Leonora. Not now, and there probably never had been.

She sat back in her chair and blinked away the tears. She had hoped against hope that her brother and her best friend would somehow work things about, but in truth she'd known all along it wasn't possible. The baby had changed things. He or she had changed things for Bob and there was no going back.

"What are you going to do?" Dorothea asked her brother. She'd thought of a hundred things she had wanted to say to him when she'd been planning this meeting. But, after his words, none of them were relevant.

Bob leant forward, took his tea cup in both hands, and looked at her.

"I need to talk to Leonora properly," he said. "And I think now is as good a time as any."

And Dorothea could only agree. So they finished their tea and she cleared away the cups and plates while her brother rang Leonora on his mobile.

From the kitchen, she could hear the low murmur of his voice even with the door shut. She was glad he'd got through to her friend and there hadn't been any need to leave a message. At her feet, Oscar purred and wound his way round her legs, and she was grateful for the comfort this simple act gave her. Dorothea couldn't help thinking that, after everything that had happened lately, Leonora was the bravest woman she knew. If she herself had been in the same position, she didn't think she would have answered her phone when she saw who was calling. And she definitely wouldn't have had the conversation that Bob and Leonora were evidently having now. She wouldn't have been able to bear it.

She had finished washing up and was starting to put away the crockery when Bob came back into the kitchen. He was frowning, but there was a sense of peace in his expression she'd not seen for a while. He leant against one of the work surfaces and gave her a faint nod.

"I've spoken to Leonora," he said. "We're going to meet up next Sunday morning. In the park. I wanted to set up an earlier meeting but she said she couldn't spare any time this week. I apologised for the way she found out about the baby. I also said sorry for the way

I've been treating her, and the way I've been handling all this. I said we needed to talk. Properly. About how our lives are going to be from now on."

Dorothea nodded back at him. She couldn't imagine this conversation would have been easy on either side, and she couldn't begin to think how painful Sunday morning would be. For them both, but especially for Leonora. She would ring her friend as soon as Bob had gone. But, right now, her brother also needed her support.

So she took the two or three steps needed to reach him and enfolded him in a hug. A proper one. She could feel the slight shake of his frame in hers and knew he was crying. Though he would never thank her if she mentioned it.

"You're doing the right thing, Bob," she whispered. "You're doing the right thing."

Chapter Thirteen

Leonora

May

It was a beautiful day. A perfect May morning. The sky was almost cloudless and Leonora could feel the warmth of the sun on her face. In the past, she and Bob had been in the habit of walking in the park on Sunday mornings whenever the weather was fine. They used to amble round the lake, and feed the ducks and swans (though Leonora was rather wary of swans and let Bob deal with them). Then they'd buy a coffee and a slice of cake at the little café to round off their visit. She'd almost forgotten how much she'd enjoyed their park walks. It was odd how they'd not been here for quite a few years. They'd stopped during Covid, of course. Nobody had been out then. But they hadn't been here for a long time before Covid either. It was funny how the things you'd always thought you'd do forever were somehow the things you left behind.

She'd been surprised when Bob had called her and asked to meet up. She hadn't known what to say, but she'd been fully prepared to end the call so she didn't have to speak with him, but there was something in the tone of his voice that made her listen. He had sounded sincere, which wasn't how he'd sounded for a long time. He'd asked her to meet up during the week, but she hadn't wanted to. She couldn't go to work and spend all day worrying about meeting with Bob afterwards. She needed the space to prepare, as she knew full well how serious any conversation now was likely to be.

So here she was, sitting on the bench near the old café which today was busy with families enjoying the sunshine, and the cakes. It looked exactly the same as it had always done, though a bit shabbier than she remembered. Leonora had told Bob to meet her here at 10.30am and it was now 10.25am. So not long to go. When she arrived ten minutes ago, she'd decided against sitting at one of the tables as there was too much noise for her to be able to think. So she'd chosen the empty bench nearest the café instead. From here, she could see Bob arrive and it would give her a few essential moments to prepare.

As she'd hoped, Leonora saw him before he saw her. This small fact made her feel a smidgeon more in control, which could only be a good thing. Her husband approached from the main park gate, hands in pockets and shoulders slightly hunched even though it was nowhere near cold. His gaze was directed at the café seating so Leonora waved to attract his attention and he came over.

"Sorry I'm a bit late," he said. "It took me a while to get parked."

"You're not late," Leonora pointed out. "It's only just 10.30am. I hope you don't mind the bench. I thought the café was too busy."

He nodded and sat down next to her. "Certainly looks it. Good decision."

A few minutes of silence and then Bob cleared his throat.

"Leonora," he said, half-turning towards her. "I want to say that I'm really so incredibly sorry for the way everything has happened this year and how very badly – appallingly in all honesty – I've dealt with it. Or not dealt with it. It hasn't been fair on you and I'm so very sorry for how hurt you've been. Hurting you was the last thing I ever wanted to do. Please believe me, on that count at least."

There were a thousand replies on Leonora's tongue, but she said none of them. Not because she didn't feel them, but because none of them would do any good. Instead she nodded.

"I know you're sorry," she replied. "You're not a mean person, Bob, and I know you never meant to hurt me. But I think what you've done and how you've done it is selfish. At best."

She thought he'd start to argue his case more, but to her surprise he didn't.

"Yes," he said quietly. "Yes, you're right. I've been selfish and I'm sorry for that too. But we do need to talk to each other, Leonora. We need to work out how our lives will be."

"Because of the baby?" she asked, trying to ignore the flash of anger and jealousy that powered through her as she spoke. This kind of emotion would do no good.

"Partly because of the baby," he said. "And partly because our lives are so different, and this is how they are going to be from now on. We need to find a way through it somehow. Please?"

Leonora had known in her heart that this was what he would say. Still, it didn't stop her taking a slow shuddering breath before she found the strength to answer.

"Yes," she whispered. "I know. *I know.* But I need a minute. All right?"

"That's fine," he said. "Shall I get us a coffee?"

Unable to speak, she nodded, and he got up, reaching for his wallet and striding towards the café. She was glad he'd given her the space she needed. He wasn't the one person in the world she could turn to with her difficulties anymore. She didn't know who that person might be but then she remembered Selena and Dotts. They were her friends and they would always be on her side. Of course they would. Even though it was hard for Dotts. But it wasn't the same as living with the person you relied on most. Being with them day to day. Not at all.

She took a deep breath, blinked away yet more tears that were suddenly threatening her and gazed round the park as she waited for Bob to return. It was odd how you could know a place and also not know it. Now, in order to focus her mind on something apart from the conversation she was facing, Leonora tried to take in as much as she could see from her seat on the bench. The water in the lake was as calm as ever, the only ripples on the surface being the slight wash from the flock of mallards slowly making their way from one side to the other. She'd never noticed how pretty ducks were, but they weren't as ordinary as she'd assumed. The males had that gorgeous green head and neck offset with a bright yellow beak. The female birds were duller but even they were speckled and dashed in their various shades of brown.

Nearer at hand were three flower beds between the lake and the café. Leonora was no expert on flower names, not like Dotts, but even she could tell that at least some of them were begonias. Like the ducks on the lake, the begonias were nothing more or less than ordinary but, even so, the colours and varieties were eye-catching. She could see reds and oranges and whites, with the occasional yellow flower popping up where it was least expected. Whether that was by accident or design would remain a mystery, but Leonora liked it. Some unknown parks employee had spent considerable time planting them all. She wished she could tell him or her exactly how much she appreciated their efforts.

Something bright and cheery was exactly what she needed.

Her thoughts were interrupted by Bob's return. He was carrying a flimsy-looking tray with two large plastic beakers and a plate of something she couldn't quite see.

As he came nearer, he gave her an uncertain smile and then placed the tray on the bench between them.

"I went for the strongest coffee they had," he said. "And I bought cakes too."

"Thank you," Leonora replied, though she was unsure whether any coffee would in fact be strong enough for her requirements.

Still, cake was always welcome, and she chose the lemon slice, leaving the chocolate muffin for Bob. She took a bite and closed her eyes, allowing the sharpness of the lemon icing to fill her senses. Then she took a sip of the coffee, which was surprisingly good. Better than she remembered it being.

Then, slowly and with not a few pauses, she and Bob had the conversation she'd known all along – since January – that they would have to endure.

They talked briefly about what had happened at the start of the year and since then, and how each of them had reacted to it. They touched upon what had gone wrong in their marriage, what might have been salvaged and what had been forever lost. At one point, they even briefly held each other's hands, as a source of comfort rather than hope.

It was Leonora who decided when they had spoken enough about the past and it was time to move on to the future. She hadn't thought it would be her, but it was. And she was, once again, glad of the small feeling of control this gave her.

"So," she said. "What happens now? After everything that's gone on, we need to move forward."

"Yes, we do," her husband answered quietly and then took a slow, unsteady breath. "Leonora, I know it's difficult, but I want my life to be with Belinda, and with our child. So I think we should get a divorce."

Yes. Yes of course. Leonora had known this was coming. She wasn't a fool. Bob had chosen Belinda over her and all the years they'd spent together, and there was no going back and no changing that choice. Not for him. And perhaps not for her either. But understanding this didn't stop his words being a shock. She had to close her eyes and think of something else entirely for a moment in order to let the facts hit home.

"Yes," she said, opening her eyes once more. "I understand that you do. And I'll go along with it, Bob. I won't put anything in your way. There'd be no point in doing so. I see that. But what about the house?"

He sighed and leant forward, putting his empty coffee beaker on the ground. "I don't know. I hadn't thought that far ahead, though I know it's something we need to decide on. But I'm not forcing you out of your home if you don't want to go. Belinda and I will manage."

"Okay. Thank you," she said. "Let me think more about it. I need time to decide."

For a while after that, they discussed whether they should use lawyers for their divorce. Bob was keener than she was to do everything right, and so Leonora was happy to agree with him. It was probably for the best. She would need to find someone local she could rely on.

And then, there wasn't much more they could say. But, from somewhere deep within, Leonora still found a kind of grace to wish her husband well.

"Bob," she said. "I know you didn't set out to be a father, but I wish you all the happiness you want for your new family. Really I do."

A deep and intense silence, and then, unexpectedly, Bob hugged her, holding her tight for a long moment before letting go.

"Thank you for that," he said, his voice hoarse. "It means everything to hear you say it. And, Leonora?..."

"Yes?"

He hesitated for a moment before speaking.

"Hell," he said at last. "It's probably top of the list of inappropriate things to say to you, but I'm going to say it anyway. On the night you discovered me with Belinda, you looked like a million dollars in that get-up, you know."

And Leonora, albeit startled, couldn't help but laugh. At the sheer chutzpah of her soon-to-be ex-husband.

Before she left the park, she saw another of those bright begonia beds next to the gate. On impulse, Leonora bent down and picked the nearest crimson flower. Then, placing it carefully in her jacket pocket, she made her way home.

Her old life had finally gone, and her new one was about to begin.

Chapter Fourteen

Selena

May

Today was the day. Max's play started its run tonight. Selena had woken up early with the absolute conviction she'd missed something vital in her costume designs. It was always like this: the colours spitting and roaring in her head and turning everything to the fiercest purple and the wildest orange. Colours she normally had no problem with, but not when the swirl and sharpness of them made her feel nauseous. She done everything she needed to do so there was no need to worry. She simply needed to convince herself of this very important point.

First of all, she'd got up, let the shower pummel away her fears, and then breathed through a ten-minute meditation. After that, she'd felt calmer. It was funny how this particular play meant more to her than just a good job done to the best of her ability in terms of the costumes. This time, her first-night nerves were deeper and more demanding.

Because of Max. Because of this man, Selena was feeling the fear not only for herself but for him as well. He'd put so much into this play. Not only money, but time and talent and vast swathes of energy. This last week had been challenging, to say the least. Every small and niggling thing that could have gone wrong in the theatre had chosen to do so. It was the unspoken law of the universe. The fridge had broken and the milk had gone off. This meant anyone not needed right then had to run to the shop to buy more at least once every two hours as no actor could survive without a constant supply of coffee. One of the scene backdrops had been torn and Grant had had to spend time he couldn't spare to mend it. Red wine had been spilt over Miss Prism's costume and Selena had needed to carry out an urgent cleaning job. Finally the actress playing Lady Bracknell had suddenly forgotten all the lines in her second appearance on stage, in spite of the fact she'd been word-perfect in every rehearsal so far.

Okay, Selena had to admit that last problem was far more serious than a mere niggle, but she was sure it was just one of those things. But it had certainly put the rest of the actors into a spin, and Max had needed to step in, make everyone take a fifteen-minute break (which meant an emergency dash to the shop for milk sooner than they'd anticipated), and then start from the beginning again when they returned.

It had all been fine then, but Selena was hoping for no more shocks today. When she arrived at the theatre at about 4pm, the real adrenaline of the opening night began to kick in. She'd attended the dress rehearsal on Sunday when everything had gone relatively smoothly. She hadn't been needed that much, apart from helping a couple of people in and out of their costumes to ensure no cues were missed.

Now, there was a distinct aura of expectation mixed with fear. The purple and orange pattern spikes were back just when Selena hoped she'd got them under control, and this time they were spattered with black. The swirling heaviness made her head throb and she gently pushed her way towards the attic through the groups of people around the stage area. She might get a few moments of peace before needing to return downstairs and check on the costume area. It was important for everything to be in the right place at the right time.

When she climbed quietly into the attic and closed the hatch behind her, Selena realised she wasn't alone. The twins were sitting at the table they'd been sitting at every Wednesday afternoon for the last few weeks and laughing together.

"Hello!" Selena said. "Lovely to see you both. I'd not expected you to be here today."

The nearest twin – who might have been Amy or possibly Poppy – turned to smile at her. The shades of lemon and grey they carried with them softened the air.

"Uncle Grant said we could come," she replied. "We've never been to a press night before, so we got permission to leave school early."

"He was busy shouting downstairs," said the other twin, peering round her sister and blinking at Selena. "So we came up here to escape. Was that okay?"

"Yes, of course it was," Selena was quick to reassure them. "And a very sensible move too. I would have done the same. Which is in fact why I'm here as well. It's quite intense down there."

Poppy and Amy smiled their agreement, and Selena smiled back.

"Are you going to think about your colours?" the twin who'd spoken first asked.

Selena stared at them both. "I'm sorry?"

"Your colours," the other twin said. "The ones which follow you around all the time. *You* know. The green and the red ones. They're very pretty."

"You can *see* them?" Selena asked pointlessly. "*Really* see them?"

Both twins nodded.

"Oh," said Selena, unsure what to do. This had never happened before in her entire life. She had no idea how to respond.

"We know you know about them," the second twin chipped in. "Because the colours talk to you and you respond."

"No, it's not talking exactly," the first twin objected. "Colours don't talk. But they tell you things. Without using words."

"That's the best way," the second twin said with a nod verging on wisdom. "Words are stupid anyway."

Sometimes that could be true, Selena thought to herself, still struggling to come to terms with the twins' revelation.

"Have you always seen colours?" she asked them, a flame of curiosity sparking up from deep inside. "Other people's? Your own?"

Poppy and Amy both shrugged. "Sure. We've always seen them. We thought everyone else did too, at first."

"But then we realised it was just us."

"Oh, and you. We realised it was you too."

"It's part of why we like coming here."

"It's comforting."

The two girls spoke in turn as if they had but one mind. Maybe that was what it was always like for twins. Selena didn't know but it wouldn't surprise her.

"Do your colours make you happy?" she asked. "Mine make me happy. On the whole. Even when they're upset or angry in some way, I like them being there. I don't know what I'd do without them. They let me be me more fully."

Poppy and Amy nodded.

"They let us be us too," they agreed.

"Good," she said, feeling far more settled and readier for the evening than she'd expected. "Now, I need to have a few moments to think and then I'll go downstairs and check everything we've been working on so hard over the last weeks. Thank you so much for all your good work, Poppy and Amy. You have a lot of talent, and I hope you know it."

They smiled at her, the lemons and greys around them turning a shade or two deeper.

"We like you too, Selena. Thank you. We'll see you later!"

And then they were gone, trotting to the attic door to take the steps downstairs. They both turned and waved at her before disappearing, and Selena was left alone.

Goodness, she thought. That was a revelation. There were others out there apart from herself who saw colours in a special way. She'd never particularly thought of herself as being alone in this gift she had. She enjoyed her life and had the best friends in Leonora and Dotty that she could ever have wished for. And now, Max. But none of them knew about her secret life. This short conversation with Poppy and Amy (or indeed Amy and Poppy!) made her feel differently about things and in a way she couldn't fully articulate.

But Selena realised, as she sat down and began to think, that the colours in and around her felt warmer and less alien than they'd ever done. Could there be more people like herself and the twins out there? And might she know some of them already? After all, she'd not realised Poppy and Amy could see colours as well, even though she'd been working with them for quite a few weeks. If this was the case, then there could be other people like herself out there whom she'd already met.

There was a thought indeed, and one that made the greens and reds in her mind swirl and dance with a quiet sense of excitement. If she was to discover this, however, then she would need to be more open about the things she saw. And that was something she'd never done in her life up to now.

Well, everything changed. Nothing in anyone's life was set in stone. She'd seen that far too well, in Leonora's life and in Dorothea's too. Nothing stayed the same for long. As for herself, hadn't she found Max when she hadn't even been looking? For however long the universe allowed them to be together. The world was an astonishing place, and you never knew what it would put into your path next. Just because she'd never shared her secret with anyone before didn't mean she couldn't at the very least consider sharing it with someone now. The very concept made Selena smile and it made her wonder.

However, she had costumes to check and, later, a play to enjoy. Her two friends would be arriving at about half-past-six which would – with a bit of luck and if the wind was in the right direction – leave them enough time for a catch-up and a quick glass of wine before the performance began at 7.30pm. They would meet Max tonight for the first time and this thought made her shiver. She hoped they would like him, and she also hoped he would like them. The meeting wouldn't last long, what with the very important matter of the play. But Selena knew how much first impressions counted, even when people said they didn't. She hoped the colours would align for them all tonight.

She was just at the attic door when a great and mighty shout reverberated up into the space and rafters around her.

"Selena, my darling! Are you up there? We need your help *now!*"

She smiled and squared her shoulders for the task.

"I'm on my way, Grant!" she replied.

For the next hour or so, Selena was involved in the general chaos of play preparation time. She'd forgotten how intense this part of the whole process could be. She dealt with last-minute costume panics, a missing shoe (nestling by a radiator for some reason) and a button determined to make a bid for freedom. She saw the twins and Grant at a distance, and even had time to share a brief kiss and a smile with Max, although he was then called for a few words with one of the invited theatre critics. She hoped everything would go well tonight. The stage area was amazing. Grant had done an inspirational job with the scenery which looked both vibrant and elegant. Their planned colours of cream, blue and gold shot through with red made the theatre sing, and the very clever lighting – not to mention the natural light from the windows – made it sparkle even more brightly.

If the standard of the play tonight matched these glorious colours, then surely the run would be a success. Selena hoped so. There was no guarantee, however, as the world of drama was an unreliable one.

A shout from the kitchen brought her back to the present and all its astonishing patterns of colour.

"Hey, Selena! Are you there?"

"Yes, I'm here, Grant. Right behind you!" she yelled back, popping up from behind a rack of costumes, and making the set designer whirl round, hands waving in the air like a mad conductor.

"Aha! You have some friends who have arrived to see you, my dear," he boomed at her even though she was standing less than two feet away. "Two fabulous ladies for our fabulous costume expert!"

"Oh good," Selena said and cast an assessing eye over the costume rail. "That's perfect timing. I think I can spare five or ten minutes before the next crisis, but if I can't, then you know where I am."

"At the bar?"

"But of course," Selena replied and gave Grant a cheeky wink.

He winked back as she left the make-do dressing room and walked out into the main theatre area.

"Oh, and Selena?" he called out just as she opened the door, the rising noise level like a wave from the ocean invading a quieter shore.

"Yes?"

"You look as wonderful as always!" he said.

She blew him a kiss and then headed to the bar, which had been set up in a corner of the room in order to find her friends. The bar staff had been hand-picked by Grant and seemed to be doing a first-class job with the space they had. On the way, she passed Iris, Max's favourite bar-owner, who gave her a bright smile and a thumbs-up, making the glorious blue colours around her dance even more brightly. No time for a chat though, as Selena had to greet her friends.

She spotted Leonora and Dorothea at once, standing together at the back and both clutching glasses of wine.

"I'm here!" she yelled and made her way through the gathering groups of press and assorted theatre-goers to reach them.

Leonora was looking stunning in a green and white suit with a darker green handbag and pair of shoes, whilst Dotts was smartly dressed in navy-blue and cream. With a cream handbag and shoes to match.

"You both look *amazing*," Selena said as she flung her arms around them and tried to hug them at the same time without causing any catastrophic wine spillages. It was quite a feat of engineering but she managed it. "Did you both buy something new for tonight? You look beautiful!"

Leonora laughed. "Yes, of course. If we have tickets for press night, then we have to buy something new. It's a law! I decided I had to treat myself, especially after how this year has been, and I found this. Not my usual style, but why not, eh?"

Selena let them go and stepped back – carefully so she didn't bump into anyone – to admire Leonora's look.

"It's perfect," she said. "Those colours really, seriously, suit you. You should wear them more often. And you look good too, Dotts. More than good. You look spectacular. Those are so very much your colours too!"

Dorothea smiled and raised her wine glass in Selena's direction. "I know. It was the obvious choice. Thank goodness for *John Lewis*."

"But we can't compete with you, Selena, no matter what we do!" Leonora cut in. "Look at how glorious you are."

Selena smiled. She'd made a big effort for tonight. It meant so much to Max and to herself too. She'd chosen a trouser suit in the wildest of wild pinks, and flattish shoes in a pale pink but with a purple stripe on them to jazz them up. Her earrings were purple studs shaped like a large star, though she was hoping they didn't fall out with all that running around she was going to be doing. Her hair was tied back with a wide pink ribbon.

"Well," she said. "I wanted to make sure the actors can find me if they need me."

Her friends laughed and then Leonora took her mobile out of her handbag.

"I must get a selfie of the three of us," she said. "For posterity."

Dotty smiled. "Oh yes. Good idea. After all, it's not often that the Friday friendship club meet up in town on a Tuesday. So we do need a picture."

"The Friday friendship club?" Selena queried.

"Oh yes," Leonora replied. "It's apparently what that bartender in the Crusting Pipe calls us, according to Dotts. She told me when we were thinking about new frocks for tonight."

"I see …" said Selena, turning to Dotts with a thousand questions on her lips.

But Dotty blushed, shook her head and refused to be drawn into any further discussion of the matter. Instead, she changed the subject entirely.

"It's a wonderful theatre," she said. "I hadn't realised this was here at all."

"It's not, really," said Selena, taking pity on her friend and deciding for once not to embarrass her. "It was originally a factory and workshop belonging to someone in Max's family. I can't remember who, but you can ask him about it later. He came over earlier in the year and decided it would be the perfect venue for the play."

"He's not wrong," Leonora replied, and Dotts nodded her agreement.

The whole space had certainly been transformed into an airy and welcoming theatre. Selena had spotted its potential on her first visit, and she'd understood what Max was trying to do, but even she hadn't thought it would be as good as this. The lack of actual stage gave the room an intimate feel even though there was plenty of space for the audience. The lighting was inviting and not too garish, and Selena particularly loved the strings of twinkling lights that had been festooned along the walls. They made tonight feel like a party, which it absolutely was of course.

"Speaking of Max," Leonora added. "I hope we'll be meeting him, even if briefly. I do understand he'll be busy."

"Oh yes," Selena replied. "He'll be focused on the press and the play, but he's looking forward to meeting you after the show, even though he knows you can't stay long. What with it not being an actual Friday and everything."

They laughed at that.

"Yes, we'll have time for a quick drink, I'm sure," Dotts said. "Though I'll need to catch a reasonable train home as I've got an important meeting tomorrow with my boss."

"Oh," said Selena. "Is it to do with the redundancy programme?"

Dotts nodded, a shadow passing over her face for a moment. "Yes, but don't worry about it. I'm sure it'll be fine. I can only do my best for the team and that's all there is to it. But never mind me. It's *your* evening, tonight, Selena, and I'm looking forward to seeing all the beautiful costumes you've made."

Selena couldn't help laughing. "And the play! Don't forget that. I hope you both have a really wonderful time. I'll catch you later."

"Yes, see you after the show," Leonora said, as she drained her glass. "Now go break a leg, or whatever it is we're supposed to say, and don't forget to have fun! I know we will."

"I'll drink to that," said Dotts with a smile.

Selena hurried back to the dressing area, aware there were suddenly more groups of invited theatre-goers milling around, chatting and drinking, than there'd been even a few minutes ago. This could only be good news for Max and the cast. In the dressing rooms, she was once again thrown back into the high-level anxiety pre-performance zone and found herself getting involved in another round of unexpected activities: searching for a lost parasol which ended up being in exactly the place it had been put in but it had been hiding under a jumper; going through a last-minute line rehearsal with the actress playing Gwendolen; and double-checking the costumes even though she'd triple-checked them a hundred times already.

It was all part of the pre-performance panic which had been going on since time began but, when Selena found Max gulping a large glass of water in the kitchen ten minutes before the start, she couldn't help hugging him. Which wasn't something she'd done to any other of the theatre producers she'd ever worked with. Absolutely not!

"It's going to be fine," she whispered in his ear as he hugged her back. "Better than fine. It will be magnificent. Just you wait and see."

She could feel the rumble of his laugh through her whole body and see the deepening brightness of the colours they shared.

"Thank you," he said. "I needed that. This all means so much more to me than I ever thought it would. I hope you're right. I hope the play will be magnificent. But I want you to know, Selena, that you're magnificent too, and I couldn't have done any of this without you. Thank you so much for being exactly who you are."

She kissed him.

"Ditto," she said with a smile and a gentle touch of his cheek. "Now, as my friends out there have just told me, go break a leg!"

The audience were settled in and the lights were already going down when Selena peered out of the dressing room door. She could see her two friends at the end of the second row of seats where she'd managed to put them. Just behind a line of media people. There was an air of expectation shimmering across the room: soft orange with flashes of green and white. Good and hopeful colours. She prayed everything would work out as Max wanted it to, and that the play would be a success. He deserved it. They all did.

A moment of utter darkness and then the lights on the stage area came up. The play had begun.

Even though she wasn't in the audience and was helping the actors with their costumes as they hurried on and off the stage, Selena could hear perfectly well how things were going. There were a few moments at the beginning when she held her breath as there was a silence she was convinced wasn't supposed to be there. Had it all gone horribly wrong? She couldn't bear the thought. Then she heard the next line being spoken (or possibly the line after it as something might well have been missed!) and the colours eased their frantic dance and cooled into lilac and grey. And she was able to let her breath go and concentrate on what she was doing.

It was surprisingly hot work, and Selena was sure she must have been drinking water every ten minutes or so. She was incredibly grateful that some unknown person had thought to fill two shelves of the fridge with bottled water as the chill of it was much appreciated. By her and by the actors. She wondered if she could get a fan from somewhere for tomorrow, but then it would probably be too noisy and would disturb the play. That was the last thing she wanted. She was much too invested in this production, and the man in charge of it, to think of doing anything which could put a proverbial spanner in the works. Tomorrow, she would simply have to wear something cooler. Goodness knows, she had plenty of options to choose from.

By the time the interval arrived, Selena was both exhausted and raring to go. The colours in her mind and in the building were dancing in glorious patterns of blue and cream, red and gold – just like the colours she and Grant had chosen for the play. She could hear the excited hum of the audience as they chatted and knew how well things were going just from the atmosphere throughout the theatre.

Max swooped in, gave her a quick kiss, and began almost at once to deliver a pep talk to the actors.

"It's going well," he said, making sure the door to the stage area was firmly shut to stop any noise seeping out. "More than well. Thank you for a sharp first half, everyone. Let's give them what they're expecting out there in the finale!"

And Selena couldn't help but smile. Max's energy created its own particular pattern of colours and shapes that helped everyone else's glow more brightly. That was Max's gift. The magical ability to encourage the talents of other people and to make something far more magnificent than the sum of what they had to offer. Just as colours and fabric were her gifts, this was his, and she was astonished she'd not seen this before. It had been there from the very beginning after all. From the first time she'd met him. She just hadn't realised it to the full until now.

If Selena had thought the first half of Wilde's play was going well, there was something about the second half which really came into its own. That was probably the way the great dramatist had written it. But there was also a magic and energy in the theatre that was entirely unique. The laughter and appreciation flowing in waves from the audience told its own story. And when the final glorious lines of the play were spoken, there came a vast ocean of applause and people whooping. From her vantage point at the dressing-room door, Selena could see that even the press row were clapping and all the colours around them were positive ones.

Closing the door quietly and while the cast took a well-deserved bow, Selena jumped up and down for a few moments and whispered an ecstatic *YES* to herself. Then she got ready to open the door for the cast to exit once more.

In the end they took three curtain calls (in spite of the fact there was no actual curtain), and she thought they could have taken at least another one too. But Max – perhaps wisely – decided it was best to leave the audience wanting more rather than less, so he brought the lights up after the third call.

Another brief interview with the press people, and then the drinks party began. Max had said he would bring everything to a close at 11pm, bearing in mind that tomorrow was another performance, but it was still good to have a quick hour to raise a glass to the start of the run and have a catch-up with everyone. Leonora and Dotts were both full of congratulations, and Selena could tell from the expressions on their faces how much they'd enjoyed the show.

"That was brilliant, just brilliant!" said Leonora. "The perfect way to spend a Tuesday."

"It was excellent," agreed Dotts, which was high praise indeed coming from her. "And I think your costumes were absolutely perfect. Well done to you all."

"Thank you," Selena said, hugging them both. "I'm so glad you could be here."

"Hello," said a familiar voice from behind her. "I'm Max. Are you Leonora and Dorothea, Selena's friends? I'm so glad you could come tonight. Thank you."

Selena spun round and gave Max a huge and welcoming smile.

"Yes," she said. "Yes. These are my very special friends. Max, meet Leonora and Dorothea. Leonora and Dotts, this … this is Max."

Her friends shook hands with Max, and then the three of them broke into smiles as they chattered about the play and how long the two of them had known Selena. The time for talking was limited, but there was something about the way the colours of the three most important people in her life met and blended that gave Selena a deep and joyous feeling of hope.

It was an important meeting and an evening to remember. For good reasons and not for bad. She could only hope that this powerful feeling of joy would help her two friends, and herself, through all the things they had to face as well. They deserved it.

Chapter Fifteen

Dorothea

May

All through the journey to work, Dorothea was thinking about Selena's play. The costumes had been magnificent and had suited Wilde's great comedy of manners perfectly. Dorothea had already known the costumes would be wonderful – she'd had no concern about that, and neither had Leonora. It was only Selena who had been on edge, as she always was. It must be the artistic temperament.

Indeed, Dorothea had had the best night out she could remember having in a very long time. Except for the Friday friendship club. That was a law unto itself.

It had even been worth the significantly fewer hours of sleep she'd been able to get and the feeling of exhaustion this morning. She'd get to bed earlier tonight to make up for it. And, in any case, Dorothea was no longer sure she had any desire to bring one hundred percent of her attention to her job. Not now the redundancy programme was in full swing. This realisation was something of a surprise. Dorothea's career had always been of very great importance to her. Now she wasn't so sure.

It was the play which had started her thought processes. What Wilde had written was full of spark and irony, with the required happy ending. But it was something else too. It was a celebration of life, an aspect of the play Dorothea had never noticed before. This feeling had come through in everything she'd seen last night: the wit of the words, the zing between the characters, the lovely costumes and even the scenery. All of it coming together in one joyous evening which had made Dorothea feel alive.

She wasn't sure if she'd ever really felt alive before. At least, not for a long time. She hadn't ever thought of it. She'd concentrated so much on her house, her garden and – most importantly – her career that the quality of being alive had never occurred to her.

Although in some ways it was quite ridiculous. She *was* alive. Of course she was. She had a good life and she enjoyed it. But was she in fact missing something? Her experience last night had raised that question. As the train continued on its unstoppable journey to the city she had worked in for so many years, Dorothea put down the book she was reading, closed her eyes instead and began to think.

Really, *properly* think.

She thought about her life and she thought about her friends. Selena first, as she always thought of Selena first whenever she thought of her friends. She was such a vibrant and powerful woman and always had been. In truth, Dorothea was sometimes unsure why they were friends at all as they were so very different. But she now couldn't imagine life without Selena. Or indeed Leonora. But she needed to concentrate for a moment or two on Selena. Her talented friend had always followed the dream she'd had to be a designer, and everything Selena had ever done had been with that end goal in view. Even the college where they'd all met for the first time had been nothing more than a stepping-stone for Selena's grand plan. Dorothea could only admire her friend for the talent she had and which she'd developed so well. Last night's costumes had been perfect. They'd suited the magic of the play as if there could be no other costumes for it. Dorothea hoped that at least some of the reviews would mention Selena's genius. They really ought to.

So Selena had followed her dream and was the most fulfilled person Dorothea knew. Did she herself have a dream, perhaps one she'd forgotten to fulfil somewhere along the road? She didn't know, but now, with her career shifting in the balance, was the time to consider this question.

Then, as the train continued its rhythmic journey, Dorothea thought of Leonora. She still couldn't help being angry with her brother, even though she loved him. She would never stop loving him, no matter what terrible things he did. And, surely, how he'd treated Leonora was the worst of all terrible things. She wondered in passing if she'd ever be able to accept Belinda fully. Each time Dorothea saw Belinda, she thought of Leonora, and so it never made for an easy interaction. She was doing her best for her brother's sake, but he wasn't making it simple.

And Belinda was very volatile too – probably one of the most volatile people Dorothea had ever met – which was again proving to be a challenge. Dorothea preferred a peaceful life, which had meant that this year was not going to be amongst her favourite years. What had the late Queen once called her worst year? The *annus horribilis*, she remembered. And she'd not been wrong.

Relationships just seemed to make everything worse. She herself had never been in a long-term relationship and she'd never wanted one. At college, there'd been a couple of short-term boyfriends and then, when she'd first started work, she'd dated one of her colleagues for a while. Though she'd never really thought of it as a full-blown *relationship* as such. After about six months, the young man in question had left for another job and that had been that. She'd not been upset and neither had he. Since then, she'd not bothered. She was more than happy on her own.

Still, Dorothea thought of the barman, Tom, but then shook her head. He was younger than she was, and she was so out of practice as to make the whole concept utterly unthinkable. Probably.

Though, in terms of Leonora, if this year showed them anything, it showed that life could change suddenly and dramatically in a heartbeat. Her friend was dealing with all these changes with courage and honesty. Could Dorothea do the same, come what may?

Dorothea didn't know, but she hoped she could. She hoped she could find her dream, as Selena had, whatever it might be. And she hoped she could handle whatever happened in her career with the kind of bravery Leonora had shown.

By the time the train arrived in London, Dorothea's mind was full of so many different thoughts and options that it was impossible to keep track of them. She needed to put them aside and prepare herself for this morning's important meeting. Perhaps things might be clearer after that.

She wondered what her team structure would look like after the meeting. Or whether there would be a team at all. What would Selena or Leonora do in such circumstances? That was easy. They would be both determined and brave, and she would have to try to show those qualities today too. For her team and for herself.

So, once in London, Dorothea squared her shoulders and made her way to the office. It was a bright morning, with that particular feeling of energy in the air that only London possessed. She'd never found it in any other city, and not in the countryside either. Today, this morning, Dorothea was glad of it.

At the front door of the building she'd worked in for so long, she keyed in her code, smiled at the receptionist and made her way to her office. Everything felt more purposeful as if it wasn't an ordinary day. Which of course it wasn't. Not at all.

She was the first of her team to arrive, and the meeting with her boss was in half an hour, before the working day properly began. She looked over her notes for the meeting once more as her colleagues arrived, and printed out a couple of copies of what she'd typed. Though she already knew it by heart.

There wasn't much chat this morning, but she had expected this to be the case. She'd got the coffee machine working and had remembered to buy a new packet of biscuits yesterday, so she made sure the team had whatever they wanted when they arrived. Whilst everyone turned their computers on, Dorothea knew not much work would be done until after the meeting, but she understood it. She would be the same in their position. She was more than glad that the boss had called her in this morning, rather than waiting until the afternoon. She didn't think she or her team would have been able to endure the tension.

Certainly, no work would have been done in that case. Though, perhaps, it wouldn't matter. Whatever her boss said, it wasn't going to be good news. In her heart, Dorothea knew it.

She arrived at her manager's door two minutes before she was due and knocked on the polished wooden panels. Instead of the anticipated command for her to enter, the door swung open and her boss gave her a quick nod as he beckoned her inside. He wasn't alone, but Dorothea had expected this. The HR Deputy Director – a blonde woman in her late thirties – was sitting at the meeting table and rose to offer her hand as Dorothea approached. For a moment, she couldn't remember the woman's name but then it came to her: Jenny. Of course. She was wearing a light floral perfume, Dorothea noticed and knew full well she was focusing on something minor to avoid thinking about the most important things.

"Well," her manager, Jack, said, and rubbed his hands together as if he was cold although in fact his office was pleasantly warm. "Thank you so much for coming, Dorothea. Can I get you a drink at all? Coffee? Tea? Water?"

"Water would be lovely, thank you," Dorothea replied and was surprised at how normal her voice sounded, in spite of the fact that her heart was beating double-time.

"I'll get it," said Jenny, and trotted off to the other side of the room where a jug of water and several glasses were resting on a tray on one of the bookcases.

While Jenny fussed with water glasses, Dorothea sat down and took out her file, a paper pad and her best office pen. Jack smiled briefly at her.

"Always so very organised," he said. "And old-school too."

Dorothea didn't reply. It hadn't been a question, and she needed to save her thoughts and words for the focus of this meeting, not the peripheries of it. She herself saw nothing wrong with being 'old-school' about how she took notes or recorded information. Writing things down on paper rather than recording them on some faceless machine helped her to think more effectively. Over the years, both her manager and the HR office had tried to persuade her to accept new technology when she was the minute-taker for any meetings, but she'd always politely declined. Jack was a moderniser in all things, and that was probably part of his role as a manager, even in the civil service. But, privately, Dorothea also thought the thrill of the new was part of his character. There was something very slippery about him, as if he was always looking for the best deal and didn't mind whom he hurt to obtain it.

This wasn't something she'd admitted to anyone else, not even her two friends. She hated gossip with a vengeance.

When the meeting started, Dorothea listened with close attention and took notes when she thought it necessary. Even though Jenny was quick to assure her that the whole meeting, which was being recorded, would be typed up as soon as possible so that Dorothea could have a copy of exactly what had been said and agreed. Dorothea simply nodded and carried on taking her notes and voicing her thoughts and opinions when asked. She suspected that what she heard during the conversation would be subtly but vitally different to what would eventually be kept as the official record. This was usually the case. In fact, Dorothea had once been at a meeting as a note-taker in the very early stages of her career when the Chair had so substantially rewritten the official minutes that the decision which had been made at the meeting was completely reversed in the paperwork.

Dorothea had been duly shocked – she hated dishonesty in all its forms – but her advice had been ignored. Apparently 'Chair's action' had been taken outside the meeting and the decision had been reversed with the agreement of all attendees. At the time, she'd wondered wryly what terrible hold the Chair had possessed over the people at the meeting, but this was something she'd not dared to ask.

As her meeting today continued, Dorothea saw clearly how her worst fears and the fears of her team were being realised. There would be no last-minute stay of execution for her office. The numbers had been crunched by the faceless managerial financiers far above her pay grade and the decision had been made. Her whole team was set to be disbanded, and the management hoped to move as many people as possible to other positions which would suit their skill sets. Dorothea made very sure they knew exactly what skill sets each of her colleagues had and made suggestions as to where they would be best reallocated. She had no idea if anyone would pay attention to her ideas, but she was determined they would at least hear what she had to say.

The progress of the meeting was to take the least qualified member of her team and then work upwards. Her own planned fate would be considered last. Dorothea didn't mind. Her focus was on the people she was responsible for, not on herself. And it was easier to find other positions for people who were at the start of their careers than it was for people such as herself. Her age – no matter what they said – was against her, as were the very specific skills she actually possessed. She could see that clearly now.

Finally, the discussion came to her own position. Jack started speaking, glancing every now and again at Jenny, but after only a few minutes, Dorothea had had enough.

"May I interrupt you?" she said.

Her manager frowned. "Yes, of course, but I do need to let you know the options."

Dorothea dismissed this nonsense with a wave of her hand. For the first time since this unexpected turn in fortunes had come upon her, she knew exactly what to say.

"I understand that," she said quietly, letting her gaze rest on Jenny and then on her manager. "But I've already made my decision. I've decided not to stay. I'll take the enhanced redundancy package you're offering. It's time for me to leave."

Chapter Sixteen

Leonora

June

Now she'd had an honest conversation with Bob, Leonora felt a thousand times lighter. It was as if she'd been carrying round an enormous weight on her shoulders she hadn't realised was there. And now it wasn't exactly gone – not entirely – but it was definitely more bearable. She still felt sad and had moments when she couldn't breathe because of the powerful punch of sadness overwhelming her. But those moments didn't last forever, and she was learning to roll with them and wait for them to pass.

It was wisdom, of a sort.

She was going to be a divorced woman, though it wasn't something she'd ever thought she'd be. She'd hoped she and Bob would be forever, but they weren't, and she had to come to terms with it. She had to come to terms with the new life she was slowly stepping into. She'd even finally managed to get herself a lawyer, though she'd not been at all sure how to go about this important step at first.

Before making the decision, Leonora had asked around at work to see if anyone knew of a decent divorce lawyer in her area. After the inevitable expressions of shock and sympathy at what she was having to go through, a couple of people – themselves divorced – had been very helpful. Even her boss – not known for having any drop of the milk of human kindness unless it was soured – had called her in to his office and said how sorry he was. He'd not offered any help, but Leonora hadn't expected it. She was surprised he'd bothered to say anything. Miracles could still happen, however small.

As a result of the advice she'd received, Leonora had chosen a local female lawyer for an initial consultation and had liked her at once. The lawyer was in her early forties, quietly-spoken, polite, but with the kind of attitude that brooked no nonsense. She'd seen another lawyer too, just in case, but Leonora had chosen the first one, and so far things were going well. That is to say, the two respective lawyers were communicating with each other, and she and Bob weren't arguing about it. Which could only be a good thing.

Her life was slowly starting again, and she was surprised to find she was feeling almost positive about the concept.

Today, Leonora was starting to prepare the house for selling. This consisted of going through each room and thinking seriously about what she needed and what she didn't. By now, Bob had removed most of his particular belongings although she was making a list of shared items the lawyer would need to ask him about. Luckily there weren't many of those, and so it was up to Leonora what she kept, what she threw away and what she thought could be recycled.

She'd assumed this clear-out would be a task she would hate. But, in fact, she was secretly rather enjoying it. Getting rid of stuff – or rediscovering stuff she wanted to keep – was very liberating. It made her feel more in control. As if her life was becoming her own, and she wasn't just part of a couple. Which, in practical terms, she no longer was. It was simply that her heart was taking longer to catch up with reality than she'd expected.

What she was more uncertain about was moving house, and finding somewhere else – somewhere much smaller – to call her own. She wasn't sure how that would work out. She'd never lived by herself. She'd been at home, growing up, and then in a flat-share when she'd started working. And then there had been Bob, and they'd been together ever since. Until now.

It was Selena who'd pointed out on one of their Friday night get-togethers that Leonora was actually living on her own anyway, and was making a damn good job of it.

It had taken a moment or two for Leonora to realise the truth of what her friend had said and then she'd started to laugh. Because it *was* true. She *was* living on her own and had been doing so since January. So perhaps living on her own in a new house wouldn't be the huge obstacle she was making it out to be. And maybe, just maybe, she was stronger than she knew or had ever imagined.

And, as Selena had carried on telling her, at least it meant she could find a home entirely suited to her needs without having to worry about anyone else. Which was, once again, something Leonora hadn't thought about. She'd thought she'd want to stay in her home forever. But now Bob was no longer there and was never coming back, the feeling of home had changed. The memories Leonora had here - the memories she and her husband had shared for so many years – were no longer purely happy ones.

Now the memories were tinged with sadness, and she could never enter a room without feeling a small punch of pain inside. Yes, that punch of pain wasn't as sharp or debilitating as it had been at the start of the year, but it was still there. And even when she caught herself smiling at some memory, the facts of the present situation didn't take long to catch up with her.

Bob had chosen a new start in life. Without her. Maybe then it was time for Leonora herself to plan a fresh start. Without him. She didn't want to move too far from where she lived now, however. She appreciated the straightforward commute to work and didn't want to jeopardise it. But there were other towns and villages in the county where getting to work wouldn't be difficult. Just as long as she was no nearer to Bob and Belinda, Leonora thought she could be happy. In fact, being further away from her soon-to-be ex-husband and his new family would be a good thing.

When Leonora had met Bob in the park, she'd not asked when the baby was due. Instead, she'd asked Dotts about it one Friday night when Selena had been ordering wine at the bar. The baby was due in August, she'd heard. So Belinda had only just been pregnant when Leonora had discovered the affair. How much and how deeply everything could change in a few months.

Leonora had thanked Dotts for telling her and even thought to congratulate her on soon being an aunt, as it was the polite thing to do. Dotts had just nodded. Then Selena had come back from the bar and the conversation had moved on.

It had taken Leonora a while to get used to the idea. She supposed it was the shock of how she'd found out in the first place. It was also partly because she'd never seen either Bob or herself as parents. So for her husband to be apparently happy to become a father had meant a re-evaluation of everything Leonora had always assumed.

It had taken a good while for her to get to grips with seeing things in a new way. At one point, she'd even asked herself, not for the first time, if everything would have been very different if she and Bob had become parents. But no, perish the thought! She didn't want children and never had – and she couldn't change that fact. Bob could change his mind as many times as he liked – or have it changed for him – but Leonora had never wanted to be a mother.

And she was incredibly glad she didn't have to be one now. She was far beyond the age of having children anyway.

So Bob had his life, and she was about to start creating her own life too. A large part of that would be her new home. And perhaps a pet. She'd always rather liked the idea of an animal in the house, but they'd never had one as Bob hadn't been keen. Something to do with not having to be responsible for it – but he would have a whole lot of extra responsibility from August, wouldn't he!

That thought made Leonora smile to herself and keep on smiling, no matter how mean it might be. She suspected her ex-husband was about to get far more responsibility in his life than he'd ever dreamed of getting, and she was quite curious to see how it turned out for him. Leonora was sure Dotty would keep her updated, at a level she could cope with.

So, a new home with a possible pet then. She wondered about a rescue dog, but she had no dog-owning skills, so it might be best to have something more manageable. A cat? No, she wasn't sure. Dotts had her cat, Oscar, but it was possible *two* cat-owning older women in a friendship group might be rather too much of a cliché. Perhaps something like a guinea pig or two might be nice. She would have to factor it into her house-buying decisions. When she got to that stage.

For now, Leonora was happy enough to sit in the living room with an essential cup of coffee and a biscuit or two, and flick through Rightmove on her laptop. It was an eye-opener, as there were more smaller and affordable houses around than she'd anticipated. Some in very good locations as well. Which was where being a local came in handy as she already knew which areas were nicer than others. She didn't have to rely on marketing blurbs for that, thank goodness.

She and Bob would need to get round to putting their old house on the market and seeing what kind of price they could get. But for now, today, looking through the kind of house which just might end up being her new home – a home of her very own! – was an utterly perfect way to spend an afternoon.

And, for the first time in months, Leonora found she had an unexpected but welcome sense of hope.

Chapter Seventeen

Selena

June

Selena understood that tonight she was going to be sad, even though she'd not been sad for some time.

The play had been a success. Which the colours had always told her, but Selena had hardly hoped to believe them. Yes, it was true to say the performance didn't have the pulling power of a West End production, but it had never set out to do that. Max's theatrical passions lay in the quirky and the thought-provoking, as it was there he felt happiest. Or so he'd told her. She understood that all too well. It was where she felt happiest too. This was one of the many things they had in common.

Those first reviews had been more than positive. Selena and Grant had been particularly pleased with the way one reviewer had pointed out the perfect blending of the play, the scenery and the costumes. Those few words had put a broad smile on Selena's face that had taken a good few hours – if not days – to leave. The colours had fizzed a brighter yellow and gold when she read this and they'd definitely taken longer to return to their usual shades. She only hoped her next project would be as enjoyable as this one had been.

Though it wouldn't have Max in it. That was an impossibility as his plan was to return to the States in about a week's time to begin preparations for another play he was scheduled to produce. This one was a very different beast – the courtroom drama *Twelve Angry Men*. An all-American play in an all-American setting. Selena thought she might have seen the film once or twice – the original one with Henry Fonda in it. Not the revamped one. It was very different from anything Oscar Wilde would have written, but none the worse for that.

In this world, there was room for all the colours one could imagine, and more. With all her heart, Selena wished there was also room in the world for Max and she to be together on a more permanent basis, but it wasn't possible. How she would miss him. Tonight, they were once again at the magical bar he'd brought her to on their first date. It was fairly quiet, with just a couple of other tables in use at the other side of the room. She wondered if anyone else would arrive though it was well past 8.30pm already. Not that she was interested in the business prospects of the pub, however much she had begun to care about the venue and its larger-than-life owner. She simply didn't want to face the darkness and sorrow of the colours to come and so was trying to distract herself. Nothing more. Selena wanted to enjoy the bright colours of the bar, sip her drink with the man she was coming to love, and make the most of their short time together. Time was, after all, the only thing they had.

"One white wine and a good British beer for me," said Max as he returned from getting their drinks.

At once, Selena put the sorrow to come to one side and smiled up at him. "Thank you. Though when did you start drinking our beer?"

Max smiled back as he sat down opposite her. "I thought I ought to sample a pint or two while I could."

Again that dark rumble of sorrows yet to be felt at the heart of the colours, but Selena shook her head to dislodge it. Some things could only be handled alone. And tonight was for her and Max.

"Good luck with that," she said. "In my very British view, it's an acquired taste."

"Cheers!" he said and raised his glass.

She took a sip of her wine and felt its oaky freshness add an essential zing to her spirit. In contrast, Max took a long gulp of his drink and then immediately looked at her in horror. He grimaced and closed his eyes for a long moment before swallowing and then starting to cough.

"What the hell *is* this?" he asked, his tone of voice distinctly higher than usual. "You guys *seriously* drink this stuff?"

Selena couldn't help but laugh. His expression was priceless.

"I think you have to be born here to love our beer," she said. "It's in the genes."

"I guess you're right," he agreed. "Honestly, it's like nothing I've ever tasted."

"I can get you something else," Selena suggested.

"A taste bud operation? That might be the only thing that can save me. But, no, I've bought it so I'll drink it. At the very least, it'll give me a feel for how you Londoners must suffer."

"Yes indeed," she said with a sigh. "After all, you've been forced to endure our appalling weather and our terrible transport system while you've been here. Not to mention our food and our television programmes. So a beer will be the crowning glory. You'll certainly never forget your stay when you've gone."

Selena had meant to be light-hearted and to keep things on that level. She hadn't meant to add the final words of her teasing reply, and she hadn't meant them to sound so serious. But when she looked across the table at Max, he was gazing at her as if he couldn't ever look away.

"Sorry," she whispered. "I didn't mean to say anything so grim and … oh, Max, I'm going to miss you so much when you leave!"

She hadn't meant to say that either, but it didn't matter. Because Max put down his glass, pushed it to one side even while she was speaking, and reached across to take hold of her hands.

"Don't be sorry," he said softly. "There's no need to be. Because I'm going to miss you too. Very much. Meeting you has been the best thing that's ever happened to me, and I don't want to lose you."

Selena blinked away tears. "But we must face facts. You have to go back to the States, Max. It's where your life is, where your job is. And my life, my job, is here. I understand that. I want you to know it's okay. Even though I love you, it's okay. I know not everything lasts forever. Let's enjoy the time we have together. It's important to make the most of it."

A silence and then Max spoke again.

"You're right in all you say," he said. "It's important to make the most of the time we have, but it's also important to make things work when there's a chance we can do that. I love you too, Selena. And I want to try to make things work out between us. The UK and the US aren't a million miles away. Not in the modern world. And, yes, my next project this summer is back home in the States, but the one after that in the fall could well be here in *your* home. Now I've made myself a working theatre in London, it would be sensible to make use of it, wouldn't it? And there are an awful lot of plays to choose from. Besides, I already know an excellent UK costume designer, and I'd be a fool not to work with her again. I want to make our relationship work, Selena. Very much. The question is: do you feel the same way?"

And, there and then and in spite of all impossibility, as the colours of despair gave way to the astonishing colours of hope, Selena knew in her heart what her answer would be.

Chapter Eighteen

Dorothea

June

Dorothea sat in her car and wondered how everything had changed so much and so quickly. Perhaps change had been heading in her direction for a long time, but she'd not seen it. She'd not been looking. She probably should have been looking and then everything would have been easier than it had proved to be. After all, she only had to consider her friends to see how change could come in an instant, whether it was good or bad.

It was hot in the car. So, as she was thinking things through, she opened her window a little and felt the warmth of the breeze on her cheek. She could hear birdsong from somewhere and could smell lavender too, although she couldn't see it. The car park wasn't full. 9.30am on a Tuesday wasn't a busy period for her local garden centre.

Leonora's change had been a bad one, that much was certain. Her marriage was over, and Dorothea couldn't help feeling sad every time she thought about it. She'd assumed Leonora and Bob were so well-suited to each other and would last the course, but she'd been proved wrong. As with so many things. She was proud of Leonora, however. In the last weeks, her friend had been doing so well, getting a divorce lawyer and sorting out her home ready for moving when the time came. She'd even been getting excited about where she might live and how she could make her new home her own. Dorothea had been impressed. It was partly Leonora's attitude that had made her own last few weeks at work more … what was the word? Not hopeful, exactly, but bearable. With a touch of hope too, she had to admit.

And look at Selena. That wonderful play with her wonderful costumes, and her new relationship with the theatre producer as well. Dorothea had taken an instant liking to Max when they'd met for the first time, and she'd seen nothing since to cause her to change her opinion. There was something about Selena that was different now. She seemed so much happier and brighter, for a start. Even though Max had headed back to the States for the summer, they were still in touch and making plans for his autumn visit to the UK. There was another play he was keen to produce here, though privately Dorothea knew the real draw was Selena. How could it not be? The last time all three of them had met up at the pub, Selena had been planning to visit Max in the States, and she had been brimming over with energy. And love too. Dorothea had smiled to see it.

Her friends definitely deserved the best. She hoped it would work out for them both.

Today, however, Dorothea had other things to consider. It was entirely refreshing to be here at this time. Usually her visits to the garden centre to restock her beloved plants were carried out on their one late opening night on a Thursday or at the weekend. But now she wasn't going up to London for work anymore, Dorothea's life had utterly changed. It had been a shock. Even though the decision to take the enhanced redundancy had been hers. Most of the rest of her team had been reallocated to other departments, which was such a relief. She was glad to hear Maddy was doing well. And Richard, who had taken the redundancy package too, had immediately accepted another job in his father's firm so that was good news.

They'd all been lucky. She missed the work and the routine, but they'd been lucky. And if there was one thing Dorothea had learnt recently, it was to be grateful for whatever luck came her way. Today, everything was different. And everything was about to change. Dorothea had spent most of her life avoiding any kind of change but here it was, and she would have to learn to cope with it. And to make the best of it. Just as her two friends had taught her in every part of their lives.

A ping on her mobile phone lying on the passenger seat drew her attention away from the day and her own thoughts. She glanced down, smiling when she saw the text.

It wasn't either Leonora or Selena. Both of them had wished her luck and all the love in the world first thing this morning, and their support was exactly what she'd needed. This message was from Tom. Her new friend from the pub. She'd given him her number on the day she'd decided to leave her job as, strangely, he had been the first person she thought of when the decision had been made. Her friends had laughed when she'd told them, but neither had said anything too embarrassing. Not even Selena.

Since then, she and Tom had been texting each other every now and again. Not too often, as that would be foolish. But just enough for Dorothea to be happy with the level of engagement. As she would have said in her career. That thought made her smile again.

"Good luck with the interview!" the text message said. *"And remember u r the best! T"*

The text-speak made her grimace but she was definitely still smiling. She sent a quick response with an added thumbs-up emoji (look at her with all this new language she was learning!) and then switched her phone to silent.

Getting out of the car, she started to walk slowly but with growing confidence towards the garden centre. It wouldn't be much of a job, not compared to her previous one, but the thought of it made her surprisingly happy. Five mornings a week doing whatever needed doing in the plant area and throughout the shop. She hoped they liked her. If they did, she couldn't wait to begin.

Epilogue

June One Year Later

For once, Leonora was on time for what she and her three friends were now definitely calling The Friday Friendship Club, or FFC for short. Which did make them sound like some kind of financial authority, but that wasn't necessarily a bad thing. After all, she'd learnt a heck of a lot more about finance over the last year than she ever wanted to know. Thank goodness her job didn't involve figures. Though, as she reminded herself as she bought a bottle of white wine at the bar and asked for the required three glasses to go with it, she'd done all right.

The face behind the bar was an unfamiliar one – much younger than Tom, but he was off travelling, this time in Scotland. Which was on his itinerary going northwards. He was on his way to take in Norway and Sweden before coming back down south and heading to Europe again. Leonora knew this because he and Dorothea were in regular contact. Not that her friend said much about it, but there was something about Dorothea's face when she talked about Tom which made Leonora smile. She wouldn't be at all surprised if Tom made his way back here in ever-decreasing circles. She wouldn't even be surprised if Dorothea decided it might be rather lovely to have a European holiday later this year. Or even a trip to see where Tom lived, in Australia. You never knew.

Yes, Dorothea was thoroughly enjoying her new job – mornings only – at her local garden centre and was even involved in some plant-based teaching activities in the centre now and again. Which she was absolutely loving. So change could happen to anyone.

Just look at Selena and her Max. A long-distance relationship, yes, since Max had gone back to the States after the success of last year's play. But Selena had been over to visit him late last summer and he'd been back for yet another play over here in the autumn. Leonora had a good feeling about Selena and Max. After all, impossible things – or things that seemed impossible – had a way of working out if they were meant to be. It was the positive side of the things that seemed possible *not* working out, like Bob and herself, for instance.

Not that Leonora was complaining that she was the only one of her three friends who didn't have a man – whether in the open or in the pipeline. After the shock of her marriage ending, and Bob becoming a father (and yes, that was still very odd indeed), she'd been surprised to find that being on her own wasn't a hugely awful thing.

Moving out of her marital home had been stressful, she remembered as she bagged a table in sight of the front door and settled the wine and the glasses in the middle. And there'd been more than a few tears over those weeks. Which Selena and Dotts had helped her to dry, even while they'd been helping her to pack.

Still, she'd found herself a cottage with a manageable and peaceful garden on the outskirts of a village not too far away from the station for her commute. It even had a bay window which was something she'd always wanted. She'd felt instantly at home there, in a way she couldn't remember feeling before. Which was strange, and made her wonder if her marriage to Bob hadn't been the settled and happy place she'd always imagined it to be. Now, she rather liked being the mistress of her own destiny. She might have been a late entrant to the world of female independence, but Leonora was determined to make the most of it. What a concept that was.

All her thoughts were instantly scattered to the four winds as a shriek of welcome came from the pub door. It was Selena, tonight dressed entirely in purple with an enormous pair of silver earrings making everything around her glitter. As stunning and as wonderful as ever.

Behind her came Dotts. Not in office get-up, but in the kind of smart casual clothes she'd started to wear more often these days and which Leonora thought suited her. She looked so much more relaxed too.

Her two special friends. How she loved them.

As they made their way over to join her, Leonora poured out a generous slug of wine into each glass and handed it to them.

"Oh, how lovely," Selena said. "Wine first and then a group hug! What could be better?"

"Thank you. Are we toasting something?" asked Dotts.

Leonora hadn't intended to toast anything, but what a brilliant idea that was.

"Yes," she said, "Perhaps we should toast something. A toast to us, I think."

"Perfect! Like we are, really," agreed Selena, raising her glass as if she were about to conduct an orchestra with it. "So. Here's to the *Friday* …"

"… *Friendship* …" said Dotts, with a smile.

"… *Club!*" said Leonora. "And to the rest of our lives too!"

"Cheers!" said Selena.

"Hear hear," agreed Dotts.

And the evening could really begin.

The End

This is a work of fiction. Names, characters, places, and incidents are either the product of the author's imagination or are used fictitiously. Any resemblance to actual persons living or dead, business establishments, events, or locales is entirely coincidental.

Cover design by The Cover Collection
Copyright © 2025 by Anne Brooke

All rights reserved. No part of this book may be reproduced or transmitted in any form or by any means, electronic or mechanical, including photocopying, recording, or by any information storage and retrieval system without the written permission of the author, and where permitted by law. Reviewers may quote brief passages in a review. To request permission and all other inquiries, contact Anne Brooke at annebrooke1993@gmail.com.

First edition
March 2025

Acknowledgements
With thanks to The Literary Consultancy for their amazing editing skills, as ever, and I am also grateful to The Cover Collection for a wonderful cover.

About Anne Brooke
Anne has been writing contemporary fiction and fantasy for over twenty years. She is the author of women's fiction novels *Three Perfect Gifts* and *The Old Bags' Sex Club,* both available at Amazon. Her website can be found at www.annebrooke.com.

More Books from Anne Brooke
Anne's Amazon page: Author.to/AnneBrooke

Any questions or comments, please email: annebrooke1993@gmail.com

One Last Thing …
Reviews, however short, are a lifeline for independent authors such as myself, and so if you've enjoyed *The Friday Friendship Club,* I would be very grateful if you could take a few seconds to let other readers know by leaving a brief review at Amazon. Thank you!
All the best
Anne Brooke

Printed in Great Britain
by Amazon